All during the day at school, Tara kept picturing the moment when she and Nate would find DeeDee's grave. Even the classes she had with Flynn, who made everything fun, never seemed to end. By the time the last bell rang, she was fired up like a roman candle on the Fourth of July. She bolted from her seat, made a quick stop at her locker, and slipped out a side door instead of taking the front, knowing full well she was going to miss seeing Flynn. She didn't have time to delay or explain, and she had a feeling he wouldn't be all that thrilled in what she was doing. He was pretty cool about her psychic stuff, but digging for bodies fell way out of the realm of normal—even for her.

The Lunatic Detective

Book two of the *Lunatic Life* Series

by

Sharon Sala

This is a work of fiction. Names, characters, places and incidents are either the products of the author's imagination or are used fictitiously. Any resemblance to actual persons (living or dead,) events or locations is entirely coincidental.

Bell Bridge Books
PO BOX 300921
Memphis, TN 38130
ISBN: 978-1-61194-043-5

Bell Bridge Books is an Imprint of BelleBooks, Inc.

We at BelleBooks enjoy hearing from readers. Visit our websites – www.BelleBooks.com and www.BellBridgeBooks.com.

10 9 8 7 6 5 4 3 2 1

Cover design: Debra Dixon
Interior design: Hank Smith
Photo credits:
Cover Art © Christine Griffin
Girl (manipulated) © Stanislav Perov | Dreamstime.com

Also By Sharon Sala

My Lunatic Life

Chapter One

Worms crawled between the eye sockets and over what had once been the bridge of her nose. The lower jaw had come loose from the joint and was drooping toward the breastbone, as if in eternal shock for the circumstance. The finger bones were curled as if she'd died in the middle of trying to dig her way out.

Tara stood above the newly opened grave, staring down in horror.

"Is that you, DeeDee?"

But DeeDee couldn't answer. There was the problem with her jaw.

All of a sudden, someone pushed Tara forward and she felt herself falling . . . falling . . . into the open grave . . . on top of what was left of poor DeeDee Broyles.

That was when she screamed.

Tara Luna sat straight up in bed, the sheet clutched beneath her chin as she stared wild-eyed around her bedroom, her heart pounding against her ribcage like a drum. All of a sudden, the loud roar of an engine swept past her window.

VVRRROOOMMM! VVRRROOOMMM!!

She flinched, then relaxed when she saw the familiar silhouette of her uncle, Patrick Carmichael. She glanced at the clock and groaned in disbelief as the roar of a lawn mower passed beneath her bedroom window again. It was just after eight a.m.—on a Saturday! Couldn't he have waited a little longer before starting that thing up?

I think you'd look great as a red-head.

Tara rolled her eyes. Millicent! She'd just had the worst dream ever and was not in the mood for any input on hairstyles from the female ghost with whom she shared her life.

"I am not dying my hair." She swung her legs over the side

of the bed and stood up.

I was once a red-head . . . and a blonde . . . and a brunette.

Tara arched an eyebrow, but resisted commenting. She'd always suspected Millicent had been quite a swinger in her day because she was still way too focused on men.

"I'm going to shower," Tara announced, and headed for the bathroom across the hall. She opened the door just as Henry, the other ghost who shared her world, came floating by. Before she could stop herself, she'd walked through him.

She swiped at her face. "Eww! Henry! I hate when that happens!"

Henry didn't appear too pleased with her either, and vaporized himself in a huff.

He doesn't like to be displaced.

"Yeah, well I don't like to be slapped in the face with frozen spider webs, and that's what that feels like."

Interesting. I remember once when I was in France—

"Millicent. Please? I just woke up here."

A pinkish tinge suddenly flashed across Tara's line of vision, then she heard a very faint pop before Millicent's voice disappeared. "Oh great. Now she's ticked, too."

Still, finally glad to be alone, Tara closed the bathroom door behind her. Just because Henry and Millicent were no longer alive in the strict sense of the word, didn't mean she wanted them as company while she showered.

A short while later, she emerged, wide-awake and starving. She dashed across the hall to her room, and dressed quickly in a pair of sweats and a new white tee from Stillwater, Oklahoma's world famous burger joint, Eskimo Joe's.

As she entered the kitchen, it was obvious from the dirty dishes in the sink that Uncle Pat had already cooked breakfast. She began poking around, hoping he'd left some for her, and hoping it was regular food and not one of his experiments.

Her uncle had a tendency to mix things that didn't necessarily go together. It was, he claimed, his way of 'going green' by not wasting perfectly good food. If she could only convince him to quit stirring everything into one big pot to heat it up, she would be happy. She didn't mind leftovers. She just wanted to know what it used to be before she put it in her mouth.

As she passed by the sink, she saw a shot glass sitting inside a cereal bowl and stopped. This wasn't good. If Uncle Pat had already started drinking this early in the morning, the day was bound to go to hell before dark. Still, after she found a plate of food in the microwave that actually looked good, her mood lightened a little. She could smell sausage and potatoes, which went well together. She just hoped the yellow stuff on the side was scrambled eggs. He'd been known to try and pass off mashed squash on her before, claiming eggs and squash were both yellow and fluffy, so he failed to see her issue. She poked her finger into the food. It had the consistency of eggs. She licked her finger, then grinned. Eggs!

"Bingo! Lucked out on this one." She popped it in the microwave to heat and poured herself a glass of juice.

With the first couple of months of her senior year at a new school behind her, she was beginning to feel like she belonged. She'd gotten off on the wrong foot with one of the cheerleaders, which had resulted in some pretty hateful gossip and hazing. When that had started, Millicent had felt an obligation to retaliate on Tara's behalf. Flying dishes and ink pens had then shifted the gossip about Tara at Stillwater High to an all-out accusation that Tara Luna was not just a lunatic, but also a witch. She could handle being both a psychic and a medium, but a witch? How lame was that?

As she dug into her breakfast, she couldn't help thinking about the one-eighty her life had taken after she'd used her psychic powers to figure out who had kidnapped Bethany Fanning, the head cheerleader of Stillwater High School. With the help of her new boyfriend, Flynn, and Bethany's boyfriend, Davis, they had managed to rescue Bethany just before she became fish food in Boomer Lake.

Just thinking about Flynn O'Mara made her shiver. He was one smooth hottie.

All in all, it had been an eventful two months.

She was still eating when she sensed she was no longer alone. Since the sound of the mower was still going strong, it couldn't be Uncle Pat. She could also sense that whoever was here wasn't mortal. She looked over her shoulder. When she saw the sad little ghost who'd come with the house they were renting, she sighed and pointed to a chair on the opposite side of the table.

"Hey, DeeDee. Have a seat. I had a dream about you last night. I've been waiting for you to come back. We need to talk."

DeeDee drifted past the chair Tara had indicated, choosing instead to hover near the doorway.

"Okay, here's the deal," Tara said, as she chewed. "Millicent explained your situation to me. I know you used to live in this house. I know you were also murdered here. I also know there was never an investigation into your murder because no one reported you missing . . . which leads me to the question, why not?"

DeeDee didn't have an answer. With a ghost, that usually meant she didn't know it. Spirits were often confused after they died. Sometimes they didn't understand what had happened to them, or where they were supposed to be. Tara knew that after the traditional 'passing into the light' they could come back and forth if they wished. But she suspected DeeDee had never crossed over. Ever. Which she found really sad.

"I'm really sorry that I don't have any answers for you, yet. But you already know I'm having problems with your brother, Emmit."

When DeeDee suddenly went from passive to a dark, angry shadow, Tara flinched. Talk about being in a mood. DeeDee was certainly in one now.

"So, what do you suggest?" Tara asked.

The dark shadow swirled to the ceiling and then down to the floor, like a puppet dancing on a string.

"That is not a helpful answer," Tara muttered, and scooped another bite into her mouth, her eyes narrowing thoughtfully as she chewed. "Here's the deal. I've already done a lot of legwork on this mystery. I found out you and Emmit once owned this house together, although he totally denies he ever had a sister."

At that news, the dark shadow bounced from one end of the kitchen to the other, rattling dishes in the cabinets.

"Easy," Tara cautioned. "No breaking dishes, please. I also found out where he lives now. You know I went to see him, which opened up this huge can of worms. Something I said to him set him off in a big way because now he's stalking me."

The dark shadow shifted back to DeeDee's ghost again, drifting about a foot above the floor like dandelion puffs floating in the wind.

"But you already knew that, too, so don't play dumb," Tara muttered. "And, thank you again for scaring him off before he found me here the other day." She frowned. "However, I still can't figure out how he got a key to this house. There's no way the lock on the front door is still the one from back when you guys owned the house. Your freaky brother either picked the lock, or had some kind of master key. Either way, he scared the you-know-what out of me . . . digging through all our closets and stuff. I don't even want to think about what he would have done to me if he'd found me hiding in the back of Uncle Pat's closet. Like I said before, I owe you for scaring him off like that. But!" She pointed her fork at DeeDee. "Did you know he's stalking me outside of the house, too?"

Tara felt the little ghost's empathy as if she'd been hugged. "Yes, well, I'm sorry, too. Thanks to you and Millicent, I've managed to get away from him both times, but my luck can't hold forever. If only you could tell me where your body is buried, it would open an investigation, and the guilty party, whom I suspect is your brother Emmit, would be caught."

Like before, an image of upturned earth and a pile of leaves flashed through Tara's mind.

"Okay. I get that the killer dug a hole, and that it was probably in the fall, because there were leaves all over the ground. But where? No. Wait. I know you were buried in the back yard." Then she grimaced. "Imagine my joy in learning that. What I meant was, I don't know where in the back yard."

Another image of the backyard flashed in Tara's mind. It was like looking at a postcard someone had sent her. In this instance, the postcard had come from DeeDee.

"I already know it's in our backyard. But it's huge. I can't just start digging holes. I don't know how deep the hole was where you were buried, or where to start looking."

Sadness swept through Tara so fast that she was crying before she knew it.

"Oh, DeeDee," Tara whispered, as she swiped at the tears on her cheeks. "I'm not giving up. I'm just talking out loud."

Within the space of a heartbeat, she found herself alone.

"Bummer," Tara muttered. "What a way to start the weekend."

She glanced down at her plate. The food was not only cold, but after the interlude with DeeDee, Tara had lost her appetite. She carried her plate to the sink, ran the leftovers through the garbage disposal, and put her plate and the rest of the dirty dishes into the dishwasher. Then she waved at her uncle, who was passing by the window again. After that, she turned, put her hands on her hips and frowned.

"Time to get down to business. There's laundry to do. The floors need sweeping and I need to make a grocery list."

Tara didn't feel sorry for herself. Her life was her life. She didn't remember anything else. She had no memory of her parents, who'd died in a car wreck before her first birthday. Her family consisted of her and Patrick Carmichael, her mother's brother—a fifty-something bachelor with an itchy foot and a gypsy soul. They'd lived in so many different states during the seventeen years of Tara's life that she'd lost count. Except for his tendency to drink too much, too often, he was a good man and good to her.

They moved to Stillwater just before the beginning of school, and if Tara had anything to do with it, they would still be here when she graduated high school next year, and still here for the ensuing four or five years it would take for her to graduate college. Oklahoma State University was one of the best universities in the state, and it just happened to be right here in town.

The possibility they might not move again so soon was better than usual because her Uncle Pat had gone sweet on a waitress at Eskimo Joe's. The waitress just happened to be her boyfriend's mother, Mona, which was a little creepy, but there was nothing Tara could do about that.

The morning passed quickly as Tara finished cleaning house. Her uncle came inside at mid-morning and helped with the laundry. They'd done it together so many times that they had their own routine.

The last load of laundry was drying and Tara was mopping the last strip of floor when Pat came back into the kitchen.

"If you make out a grocery list, I'll do the shopping," he offered.

"Yay!" Tara said. She hated grocery shopping. "Give me a couple of minutes to finish up here and I'll get right to it."

"I'll be outside," Pat said. "I need to clean out the trunk of the car anyway."

"Okay," Tara said, as she put up the mop.

She went back to the counter and picked up the list that they'd started earlier in the week and began sorting through the pantry and the refrigerator, making notes of the things that needed to be replaced while absently dancing to a little Katy Perry playing on her iPod.

The front door had barely shut behind her uncle before Millicent popped up.

You're out of shampoo.

Tara looked up from the list and frowned. "And you know this because?"

There was a small accident in the bathtub.

Tara dropped the list onto the kitchen table. "Dang it, Millicent. Have you been making bubbles again?" She stomped off to the bathroom, muttering under her breath as she went. "I don't know why you persist in this when you know good and well you can't do bubble baths anymore."

Tara squealed as she ran into the bathroom, turned off the water running into the tub, then pulled the plug to let it run out. Of course, it was too late to stop what had already overflowed.

"Look at the mess you've made!" she shrieked. "You explain all this to Uncle Pat, will you? This stuff costs money, and we're not rolling in it, in case you've noticed."

Money? Isn't that what you got for finding that blonde bimbo?

Tara ignored the remark regarding the reward she'd gotten for finding Bethany Fanning, because that was going to be her ticket to four years of college. She sighed as she surveyed the partially flooded bathroom floor.

"I hope you're happy. I had just mopped this."

Sarcasm does not become you.

Tara knew her little ghost was gone, even before the sound of Millicent's voice disappeared.

"Henry! Why didn't you warn me?" Tara wailed, as she went to get the mop and bucket again.

Henry manifested long enough to blow her a kiss, then vaporized.

Tara wasn't amused. It seemed everyone had a place to be but her. She finished cleaning up the bathroom—again—and ran back to get the list before her uncle came back. She didn't want to explain why she was mopping the bathroom twice. Even though he'd finally accepted the fact that she was as psychic as the other women in his family had been, he didn't like to dwell on it.

She added a couple of other items to the list and hurried outside, only to find him engrossed in a conversation on his cell phone. From the laughter in his voice and the little she could hear, she guessed he was talking to Mona. When he saw Tara, he quickly said goodbye and stood.

"Got the list?" he asked.

Tara slipped it in his hand. "Are you going out with Mona tonight?"

He blushed. "I don't know ... I might. Is there a problem?"

Tara sighed. "Flynn and I are going bowling."

"That's great," he said.

Tara shrugged. "You don't think it's weird? I mean, I'm going out with Flynn and you're dating his Mom?"

Pat frowned. "I fail to see the problem. I'm just taking a woman to dinner. We're not getting married. Flynn's not going to turn into your step-brother overnight."

"Ew! Ew! I hope not!" Tara cried. "How wrong would that be? All of us living under the same roof?"

Pat hugged her. "Honey, that is so far down the road of ever happening that you need to calm down. Dinner and a movie is not forever after, okay?"

Tara sighed. "Yeah, okay."

"So, I'll be back in a couple of hours. Kick back and take a good rest. I've got the back yard all cleaned up, but I've been thinking about putting in a small mum garden. You know . . . they're colorful and hardy and good to plant this time of year. Why don't you poke around and figure out a good place for us to plant them?"

Tara immediately thought of DeeDee. "Great idea, Uncle Pat. I'll do that."

He tweaked the end of her nose, then winked. "Okay. I'm leaving now. Later gator."

Tara rolled her eyes as he got in the car and drove away. Uncle Pat was a hoot with his funny old-time sayings.

Where are you planning to dig first?

Tara rolled her eyes. "Here's the deal, Millicent. It's not like you can just start digging holes. Our landlord would toss us out for tearing stuff up."

Tara went back into the house and locked the door firmly behind her as Millicent continued.

Then how are you going to find DeeDee?

"I don't know, okay? I'm going outside now, and if I'm real lucky, DeeDee will pop up, point her little ghostly finger and say 'X marks the spot.'"

As I have stated before, sarcasm does not become you.

Tara sighed. Great start to her Saturday. She'd displaced some of Henry's molecules, ticked Millicent off, and made DeeDee sad. And that was only the ghost side of her troubles.

Uncle Pat had a date with Flynn's mom. What if there was hugging and kissing involved? What if they actually hooked up? OMG. OMG.

Her feet were dragging as she headed out the back door, then paused on the bottom porch step with her hands on her hips.

"Okay. If I wanted to hide a body out here, where would it be?"

A picture popped into her head and she realized it was another 'postcard' from DeeDee. Just as she started to dismiss it, she realized what she was seeing wasn't what the back yard looked like now. It was different. Decidedly different. The back yard fence wasn't chain link, it was wood, and roses were climbing up the trellises against it. There was a circle of irises around a birdhouse on a pole, and a vegetable garden in the far north end. And there were morning glory vines all over the side of a shed that was no longer here.

OMG. DeeDee was showing her what the back yard used to look like.

"Okay, DeeDee! I get it. Keep it coming. I see it. Trees. There were big shade trees. And before you showed me a pile of leaves. I remember. I remember."

Tara leaped off the step and started out across the yard, following the old stone path that wound through the yard. Now the path even made sense. It had led to different parts of the garden.

As she walked, she couldn't imagine the depths of depravity it would take to kill someone, let alone a member of your family. And even though she didn't know who had killed DeeDee Broyles, her brother seemed the obvious culprit. He had denied ever having a sister, then broke into Tara's house and was still stalking her. It wasn't looking good for Emmit.

She wondered what the prison system did with old men like him. Was there a senior citizens wing in the penitentiary? Did they still draw Social Security and get retirement checks? How weird was that?

Tara was lost in thought as she followed the path, trying to figure out where someone could dig a hole big enough to hide a body and make sure no one found it when she realized she'd been looking at the answer all the time.

The fence. It used to be tall. Wood. All around the yard. No one could see over. No one could see through.

OMG. You could dig holes all over and no one would know it. You'd have all the time in the world to plant bushes or shrubs, or anything you wanted to hide the fact that earth had been overturned.

She stopped, put her hands on her hips and turned around, looking back toward the house. Uncle Pat wanted her to find a place to plant some mums. She wanted to find a body. Both required digging holes. Piece of cake.

Henry suddenly popped up in front of her, waving his hands.

Tara frowned. "What's up? Don't tell me Millicent is making bubbles in the bathtub again? No? Uncle Pat? Something happened to Uncle Pat?"

I think he's trying to tell you someone's coming down the alley.

Millicent's explanation wasn't warning enough. Tara pivoted just in time to see a car coming down the alley between the houses. No one was supposed to drive through there except maybe city employees. Then she realized she'd seen that car before—and the man driving it.

It was Emmit Broyles.

Oh crap! He was doing it again. He was still stalking her.

She started to run toward the house, when she realized it would give away the fact that she was scared of him. So far, Emmit didn't know she was on to him. She remembered reading once that the best defense was an offense so she lifted her hand and started waving as she moved toward the alley.

"Hi, Mr. Broyles," she cried, and jogged toward the fence, as if expecting him to stop.

The look on his face was priceless. His bushy white eyebrows shot upward as if someone had tied strings to them and given them a yank. He must have tried to stomp on the accelerator, but he was obviously distracted enough that he missed and stomped the brake instead.

All of a sudden he was flying forward. His chin hit the steering wheel and the hat he'd been wearing shot off his head and landed on the dash.

"Are you all right?" Tara yelled, as she neared the fence.

Even though all the windows were up, she could tell he was cursing at the top of his voice. He grabbed his hat, shoved it back on his head. Ignoring the blood dripping from his chin, he finally found the accelerator and roared off down the alley.

Tara grinned.

I think that went well.

Tara's smile widened. "Yeah, it did, didn't it?"

She turned around to go back to the house only to realize DeeDee was standing right beside her.

"Oh. Man. You did it again, didn't you?" Tara asked.

DeeDee disappeared.

"So, obviously we're not discussing this."

How would you feel if your brother was the one who ended your life?

Tara's smile died. "I never thought about that."

Because you never had a brother?

"No. Because I didn't think how DeeDee would take the news. I guess I just assumed they didn't get along."

You know what they say about assume. It makes an—

"Yes, yes, I know. An ass out of u and me. Very funny."

Tara heard the phone ring and sprinted toward the house. She was slightly out of breath when she answered.

"Hello?"

"Hey, Moon girl, I must be getting better by the minute. The mere sound of my voice has left you breathless."

Tara laughed out loud. "You are too funny," she said. "I was in the back yard looking for . . . uh . . . I was in the back yard."

"So, are we still on for tonight?" Flynn asked.

"Absolutely," Tara said. "We're going bowling, right?"

"Yeah, unless you'd rather do something else?"

"No. No. I love to bowl. I'm not very good, but it's fun."

"Good. How about some Hideaway pizza before we go?"

"Oh, yum! I've heard they make the best."

"Oh, yeah," Flynn said. "So I'll pick you up about six, okay?"

"Yes."

Tara started to hang up, then thought of his mom and her uncle. "Hey, Flynn?"

"Yeah?"

"Did you know your mom and Uncle Pat have a date tonight, too?"

There was a moment of silence. Then a chuckle. "No, but I'm cool with it. Aren't you?"

"Oh, it's not that. It's just . . . kind of weird."

"You think too much, Moon girl. Let the old folks have their fun."

Tara laughed. "See you at six."

Chapter Two

Tara was pumped. Uncle Pat had come back from shopping with a surprise for her—a new red and black knit top and a black hoodie to match. She tried it on immediately and squealed with delight that it fit.

"Way to go, Uncle Pat," Tara said, as she modeled it for him.

Pat frowned as he eyed her. "Where did the years go? It seems like only yesterday that you were still learning how to tie your shoes."

Tara gave him a nervous glance. "You're not gonna go and get all squishy on me, are you?"

"No. Of course not," he blustered, then sighed. "You just make sure that Flynn O'Mara keeps his hands to himself."

Tara was horrified by the turn in conversation and rolled her eyes. "Please. I know how to behave, okay?"

"Did I question your behavior? No. I did not, thank you. I trust you, honey. I just don't know that boy well enough to know if he's trustworthy or not, and neither do you."

Tara sniffed with indignation. "Yes, well, the same could be said for you, too, you know."

"I'm sure, uh, it doesn't mean . . . Oh. Never mind. I need to finish putting up groceries."

"And I need to wash my hair."

Agreeing to disagree on the subject of the O'Mara family, they went their separate ways.

A few hours later, Mona and Flynn were at the door. Pat left in his car with Mona, leaving the O'Mara vehicle for Flynn and Tara to use.

"That was weird, sending them off on their date as if we were the parents and they were the kids," Tara said, as Flynn slid behind the wheel and started his car.

He grinned. "Kinda. But I have to admit, it's good to see my Mom happy again."

Tara nodded. "Yeah, I know what you mean. Uncle Pat hasn't done this in ages. Maybe since I was thirteen or fourteen."

Flynn gave her an appreciative look. "I don't know how you looked at that age, but you're dang hot now, Moon girl. Nice outfit."

Tara grinned and made a mental note to thank Uncle Pat again for her new clothes. "Thanks."

Flynn pulled out into traffic, then gave her hand a quick squeeze.

"Hope you're hungry."

"Starving," Tara said.

In my day, we never admitted to being hungry.

Tara frowned and gave Millicent a silent warning. *,OMG Millicent! We are not doing this. Get lost.*

Don't worry. He'll never know I'm here.

But I will.

Yes. Well. There is *that.*

Tara stifled a snort. If she didn't know better, she'd think Millicent and Uncle Pat were in cahoots about her dating.

"What's your favorite kind?" Flynn asked.

Tara blinked. She'd been so focused on her mental argument with Millicent, it took her a few seconds to shift gears. "Um . . . of pizza, you mean?"

Flynn arched an eyebrow. "Well, yeah. What else would I be talking about?"

Dang it, Millicent! See what you do to me? She shrugged and smiled at Flynn. "I don't know. I'm just being silly. As for pizza favs, I only like two kinds."

Flynn frowned like he hadn't expected her to be picky. "Okay. So, what are those?"

"Hot pizza and cold pizza," Tara said, and then grinned at the expression on Flynn's face.

"I set myself up for that, didn't I?" Flynn said. "But that's good, because those are my favorite kinds, too."

A short while later, they were walking into The Hideaway. Like Eskimo Joe's, it was something of a Stillwater landmark. And Tara could tell from the banging in the kitchen and the low buzz of conversations from the hungry patrons, things were hopping.

"Yum," Tara said, as Flynn guided them toward the hostess. "Smells great in here."

"So do you," Flynn said, then grinned when he saw her cheeks turn pink. "Are you blushing?"

"Absolutely not," Tara said, but she was still smiling as the hostess led them to a table.

"Hey, there's Davis and Bethany," Flynn said, pointing to a table on the other side of the room. "They're waving at you."

Tara looked. "They're waving at us," she corrected, and waved back before taking a seat.

Tara couldn't help but notice a family of five at a table across the aisle as she and Flynn sat down. The kids didn't know how lucky they were to have both parents doting on them and making sure they had everything they needed, including love. It wasn't like she was hurting for attention, but having a Mom would be so cool.

"Hey, earth to Moon girl."

Tara blinked. "I'm sorry. Were you talking to me?"

Flynn nodded. "No big deal. Just wanted to know what kind of pizza to order."

"Sorry." She grabbed the menu and started to scan it, then rolled her eyes and put it down. "I couldn't make a decision if I had to. Order something. I promise I'll help you eat it."

Flynn laughed. "Want salad or anything to go with it?"

"No, thanks. I'm a purist. Oh, and I'll have Dr. Pepper, please."

Flynn lowered the menu to look at her. He kept looking for so long Tara got nervous.

"What?" she asked.

"Nothing," he said, and went back to the menu, but Tara got the message. He was into her big time. That was all good.

His thoughts are impure, you know.

Millicent!

Whatever.

Tara sighed, thankful for small favors when she felt Millicent zap out again.

A short while later they were both digging into a large three-meat pizza with extra onions and peppers. Flynn was eating two pieces to Tara's one without apology, but the coolest thing about the evening so far was that Flynn was easy to be around.

Tara was reaching for her third piece of pizza when she felt the air around them changing. Within seconds, she realized it was the same dark feeling she'd had walking into school with Flynn right after they'd rescued Bethany Fanning. Someone close by not only didn't like her, they wanted her gone. As in dead.

She shivered as she looked up. wondering if Emmit was there. She didn't see him, although there were a couple of other dining areas in the restaurant. Not hungry anymore, she dropped the pizza back onto the pan, then wiped her hands on her napkin.

"Um, Flynn, where's the restroom here?"

"Oh. Sure." He turned around, then pointed. "Over there. See that little sign?"

"Thanks. I'll be right back," Tara said, and then pointed to the swiftly disappearing pizza. "Save me one more piece, okay?"

He grinned. "If you hurry."

Tara smiled, then headed for the restroom, but as soon as Flynn turned back around, she slipped through the arch into the dining area on the other side and scanned the room. It was full to overflowing with a line of people still waiting to be seated, but no Emmit.

She couldn't figure out who would have a grudge against her so strong that it would elicit this kind of hate.

"Can I help you, hon?" the hostess asked.

Tara turned. "Um. No, I'm fine. I was just looking for

someone," she said, and then turned around and headed back to the table and Flynn.

"That didn't take long," Flynn said.

"I was afraid you'd eat all the pizza," Tara said, and just to prove her point, grabbed that third piece and slipped it on her plate. Then she reached for the red pepper flakes.

Flynn's eyes widened in appreciation as he watched her liberally sprinkled them all over her pizza slice.

"Want some?" Tara asked.

"No thanks," Flynn said. "I want to still be able to taste mine."

Tara grinned. "I like spicy stuff. Comes from living in New Orleans. And Savannah. And Carmel, and Denver and—"

"Dang, Moon girl. Are you serious? Have you really lived in all those places?"

"And then some," Tara said.

"I was born and raised in Stillwater. Never lived anywhere else."

"Lucky you," Tara said. "It's not fun always being the new kid in school."

Flynn frowned. "Yeah. Never thought of it like that. I was just thinking of all the country you and your uncle have seen."

"Yes, but here's the sad part. After a while, all the cities and towns start to look alike."

"Why do you keep doing it, then?" he asked.

Tara shrugged as she took a big bite and chewed thoughtfully. "I always think of Uncle Pat having an itchy foot and a gypsy soul, but the truth is, I think he's just never found anyone worth staying around for."

"Maybe this time will be different," Flynn said.

"If I have anything to do with it, it will," she said. "I would love to go to OSU. How about you?"

He nodded. "Living at home and going to college will be the only way I can ever swing it, so yes, I'm planning on going to school here."

"What do you want to be?" Tara asked.

Flynn didn't answer quickly, and almost immediately, Tara

picked up on why. His Dad. He wanted to go into Criminal Justice and his Dad was in the pen. How ironic was that?

"I'm not sure what my field of study is going to be," Tara said quickly, hoping it took the pressure off of him having to come up with an answer that didn't embarrass him. "I mean, what kind of a career can I have and still be me?"

Flynn's eyes narrowed as he realized she was talking about that psychic side of her.

"So, isn't there something you could do that would utilize your, uh, skills?"

"Hmm, let me think? Fortunetelling? No. I could be a therapist and speed treat patients by cutting through all their baloney and getting to the real problems underneath. I'm sure that would make me super popular. Or I could be a human lie detector for the FBI. Or work for a big city police department with lots of unsolved murders. The ghosts can tell me their stories and I'll pass them on to the police. Who will, of course, believe me when I tell them I talk to ghosts and read minds."

He laughed out loud. "I see your point."

Tara grinned. "I'm glad you find that amusing."

"Sorry," he said. "It's just, I don't know . . . it's just amazing what you do and I'm sort of in awe."

That's cause he wants to kiss the pizza off your face and—

Millicent!!! Get lost, Tara thought, and then wiped her mouth quickly. "Ooh, that was so good, but I'm stuffed. You were right. The Hideaway's pizza is totally the best ever."

Flynn grinned. He was still smiling at her when she felt something that made it impossible to smile back.

Someone was dying.

The spirit of a little boy was suddenly hovering in the air over a table, looking down. It was the little boy from across the aisle.

Without giving herself time to think, she bolted out of her chair and caught the little boy's body just as he began sliding lifelessly out of his booster seat. She didn't have to do the normal methods of CPR, checking for a pulse or signs of breathing, because she already knew he had neither. She also knew without having to look that something was lodged in his windpipe.

"He's not breathing!" Tara cried, as she flipped him over, balancing him tummy side down on her arm, with his chin resting in the palm of her hand. Quickly, she braced the baby and her arm against her leg then began hitting him between the shoulder blades.

Once. Twice. Three times she whacked the child in the middle of the back while his Mother was screaming in her ear, and his father was trying to grab the baby out of her arms.

"Don't! Don't!" Tara cried. "He's not breathing."

Then the mother focused on the baby's face and saw that he was already turning blue. She screamed. "Robby! Robby! Oh my God, Beau, she's right! Robby's not breathing."

Tara repositioned the baby once again and then gave him another sharp whack in the middle of the back, unaware that the room had gone silent. It was as if everyone was holding their breath along with the child who couldn't breathe.

Please, God, don't let this little boy die, Tara thought as she hit him once more. Then suddenly something popped out of the little boy's mouth and onto the floor. Within seconds, the toddler began to wail.

Tara pulled him upright, then sat him down on the side of the table. From the way he was crying, it was obvious his airway was no longer blocked. Now that the danger had passed, she felt weak in the knees.

"I think it all came out," Tara said, and set him in his mother's lap.

"Oh . . . thank you, thank you," the mother said, as she ran her hands over the little fellow's face. Then she clasped him to her and looked up at Tara. "How did you . . . ? I didn't know he was—"

Tara just pointed to the floor and the round black olives that had popped out of the little boy's throat.

"I saw him put them in his mouth. He didn't even chew them," Tara said. "That's why they got stuck going down."

The father was horrified. "He loves grapes. He probably

thought they were grapes." Then he grabbed Tara's hand and began thanking her again and again.

Now that it was over, Tara was a little embarrassed and worried what Flynn would think. She'd made such a scene, he would probably—

Flynn put his arms around her and gave her a big hug.

"Way to go, Moon girl," he said softly.

Tara sighed. It was going to be all right, after all. She slid back into her chair without looking around, although she could hear people all over their dining area praising her quick thinking.

They all thought she'd seen the little boy put the olives in his mouth. She hadn't seen the child do anything but go airborne over their table. If they knew what she'd really seen, they would surely freak.

Moments later, the manager of The Hideaway appeared, making sure that the parents didn't require emergency services. Once he was satisfied all was well, he shook Tara's hand, then picked up the ticket the waiter had put on their table.

"Your dinner is on the house." He patted Tara's back once before walking away.

"That was cool of him," Flynn said.

Tara rolled her eyes. "Can we leave now?" she whispered, anxious to get away from the curious stares.

"Absolutely," Flynn said.

The best thing was that he had his arm around her shoulders all the way out the door, which told her in more than words that he wasn't embarrassed by what she'd done. They got all the way to the car before Flynn spoke.

"You are amazing," he said softly, then slid his hands beneath the hair at her neck and kissed her.

Tara sighed, then leaned into the kiss. He tasted like pizza and Coke and Flynn, a lethal combination. When he finally pulled back, they were both a little rattled by the intensity of the moment.

"Flynn . . . I—"

"Ready to go bowling?" he asked.

Thankful he'd changed the subject, she managed to nod.

"I can't wait to see what you do for an encore," he drawled.

Tara doubled up her fist and punched him on the arm, and the tension of the moment was gone. But even as she was getting into the car and closing the door, she felt the remnants of the hate she'd felt before the little boy choked on the olives. She looked over her shoulder as Flynn pulled away from the curb, but, like before, saw nothing suspicious.

"You okay?" Flynn asked.

Tara turned back around and made herself smile. "Yes, great." She'd had enough drama for one night. She hoped it was over.

"So we're off to Frontier Lanes," Flynn said. "It's on the way out to Boomer Lake, and I think I should warn you, I'm pretty good."

Tara grinned. "I think I should warn you . . . I'm not."

Flynn laughed out loud and Tara shivered. He was so cute when he did that.

And I think I should warn you I'm back.

Tara resisted rolling her eyes. *Of course you are. Just when the going gets good.*

It is my intent to make sure nothing goes too far or gets too good.

Great. *Good grief, Millicent. You're as bad as Uncle Pat. What do you think I am?*

Human.

Oh.

I rest my case.

"Are you all right?" Flynn asked.

Tara jumped. It was a little difficult to juggle a silent conversation with a ghost and a real one with a hottie.

"Yes, sure. Why do you ask?"

"You just got all quiet. Thought you might still be a little shook about that kid."

"I might have been quiet in the car, but I was not quiet in my head."

Flynn frowned. "What do you mean?"

Tara sighed. "You don't want to know."

Flynn stopped for a red light, then glanced at her profile. "You know something? I just realized you look a little bit like Angelina Jolie."

Tara's eyes widened and her mouth made a perfect little O. "You have just made my day. She's my absolute favorite actress ever."

Flynn grinned. "Glad to oblige. She's pretty hot, too."

Tara blushed when she realized he'd just implied that both she and Angelina were hot.

"I guess," Tara said. "But the reason I like her best is because she adopts babies that no one else wants."

The smile slid off Flynn's face as he got it. "Sorry," he said softly.

Tara frowned. "Why? You don't have anything to be sorry for."

He shrugged. "I keep forgetting it's just you and your uncle."

Tara nodded.

"No grandparents? Aunts? Uncles? Not even some cousins?"

"Nope," Tara said. "How about you?"

"Mom's parents live in Lawton. That's south toward the Texas border. Dad's mother is still living, but she's in an assisted living center in Oklahoma City. She's had a couple of strokes and isn't well. Mom has a brother and a sister, and my Dad has two brothers. I have cousins all over the place, but not in Stillwater."

"Do you see your family often?"

"We try. The deal is, we know they're there. After meeting you, I've begun to realize how lucky I am, and that I'm wasting some precious time that I might not be able to get back by assuming they'll always be there."

"Yeah. You should visit them when you can, especially the older ones," Tara said.

There was as long moment of silence between them before Tara broke it with a question that had been on her mind for days. She knew Flynn's father was in prison for burglary, and she knew his parents were divorced. And during the hunt when Bethany had gone missing, she'd picked up on the fact that Flynn's father had cancer and told him she knew. They'd never spoken about it again.

"Flynn, can I ask you something?"

"Yeah. I guess," he said cautiously.

"It's about your Dad."

He made a face.

"Have you told your Mom about his cancer?"

Flynn sighed. "No."

"Are you going to?"

He shrugged, and then braked for a stop sign before turning right. He didn't answer.

Tara frowned. "Sorry. I didn't mean to intrude. It's just that I've been thinking about it, and wondering what I would have done in your place. That's all."

Flynn's eyes narrowed, and then he signaled to shift lanes before finally turning off the streets and into the parking lot of the bowling alley.

"We're here," he said, as he put the car in park and killed the engine. Then he grabbed Tara's hand to stop her from getting out. "Wait. I wasn't ignoring you. I just don't know how to answer, because I haven't decided what I should do."

"It's not really my business, and I'm sorry I asked," Tara said.

"No. I think maybe I need someone else's input here. If you were me, what would you do?"

Tara thought for a couple of moments, then turned sideways in the seat until she was facing Flynn.

"Did your parents really love each other?"

He nodded. "Yeah. I think Mom still loves him, but he nearly destroyed us, financially and emotionally, when he got hooked on Meth. That's why he started stealing. To pay for his drug habit. Mom didn't divorce him until he finally went to prison."

"Then I'm thinking she would want to know. I'm thinking that if there was unfinished business between them, that it would be really sad that she never got a chance to ... to ... I don't know ... maybe tie up loose ends? Do you know what I mean?"

Flynn nodded. "I never thought of it like that. Thanks, Moon girl. Mom's off tomorrow. I'll talk to her then." Then he grabbed her hand. "Let's go in. I'm feeling real lucky tonight."

Nobody gets lucky on my watch.

Tara laughed.

Flynn grinned, thinking she was laughing with him.

A short while later, they had their bowling shoes on, an alley assignment, and were picking out bowling balls.

GET THE RED! I LOVE RED!

Millicent's voice came unexpectedly, making Tara jump. She almost dropped the bowling ball she was testing onto her foot. *Can you please not shout in my ear?*

Sorry. I just got excited.

"Did you find one that feels good?" Flynn asked.

Do not answer that.

Calm down, Millicent. He's talking about bowling balls.

Oh. My dad.

Tara rolled her eyes. *It's not my dad. It's 'my bad.'*

I do not err.

Tara chose to ignore Millicent's last remark and focused on Flynn instead.

"I think this one will work." She carried the ruby red bowling ball to their lane and put it in the rack.

"You go first," Flynn said. "Throw a couple of warm-up balls."

"Okay," Tara said. "But I'm warning you, this may prove embarrassing. To both of us."

Flynn grinned as he slid into the scorekeeper's seat. "It's all in good fun, Moon girl. No pressure. Okay?"

She nodded, picked up the red bowling ball, and took her position at the front of the alley. Her first ball went a little bit airborne, then hit the lane with a thump before wobbling halfway down the lane and ending up in the gutter.

"I warned you," Tara muttered, as she turned to look back

at Flynn. "Wipe that grin off your face, mister."

He chuckled. "I can't. You're too cute when you're ticked."

Tara stifled a smile and then caught her ball as it returned, and gave it another try.

Tara's ball actually spun down the lane with decent speed and took out six pins. "Hey, Moon girl, way to go," Flynn said.

Tara grinned. "That's what I'm talking about," she said, and traded seats with him. "Your turn to warm up." She gave his backside an appreciative look when he bent over to release his ball.

I saw that.

Tara grinned. *So did I, thank you very much.*

And so their game began. By the time they were ending their third and final game, Tara knew she was in serious like with Flynn O'Mara. And at the same time that revelation hit, she felt a dark, sick hate pouring through her body.

She grabbed onto the back of her chair to keep from staggering, and then turned around to look behind her. Before she could focus, she started to faint.

Chapter Three

Nausea rolled through Tara so fast she thought she was going to throw up.

You need to get out.

Tara heard Millicent's warning, but she couldn't move. Instead, she staggered, then slid down into a seat and put her head between knees. She didn't see Flynn drop to his knees in front of her, but she heard his voice in her ear.

"Tara! Tara! What's wrong?"

She mumbled something incoherent, and he quickly felt her forehead. She knew she didn't have a fever.

"Did something you ate make you sick? All those red pepper flakes?"

She shook her head without lifting it.

"Moon girl, talk to me," he begged.

"Someone . . . someone wants me . . . dead," Tara whispered.

"What the hell?" Flynn stood abruptly, scanning the crowded bowling alley, looking for something—anything. "What do I need to do?"

"Out. Get me out."

Flynn yanked the rented bowling shoes off her feet and tossed them in the seat, then slid her feet into her shoes. Moving frantically, he slipped his hands beneath her arms and pulled her upright.

"Lean on me," he said urgently, and together, they started toward the door.

Hurry, Tara, hurry.

Tara's head was down, her eyes were closed, and even though she could hear Millicent's warning, she staggered more than walked.

They were more than halfway to the door when someone came up behind Flynn. It was Nikki Scott and her boyfriend Corey Palmer.

"Flynn! What's up with Tara?" Nikki cried.

"Help me get her outside," Flynn said.

Corey got on the other side of Tara and quickly slid his arm around her waist. At that point, her feet left the ground as they carried her toward the door. Nikki ran ahead to open it.

Tara was numb. She knew she was moving, but she couldn't focus. She couldn't even call out for Henry or Millicent. Never in her life had she felt this helpless.

The wind had come up since they'd gone into the bowling alley, but she needed more than fresh air to recover.

"Are you feeling any better?" Flynn asked, as he and Corey got her to his car.

"Purse . . . in the—" Tara mumbled.

Nikki held up the little shoulder bag Tara had with her. "I've got it."

No. No. That wasn't what she meant. But she couldn't get the words out of her mouth in the proper order. Too many thoughts flew through her mind. She kept getting flashes of someone with a scar on his face and blood all over a floor. Screams, one after another, echoed inside her head.

Flynn unlocked the car and they quickly slid her into the passenger seat.

"Are you gonna take her to ER?" Corey asked.

"No . . . not hospital . . . purse. Need . . . purse," Tara said.

Nikki gasped. "I think she means there's something in her purse she needs." She started digging through it, looking for something obvious, like a bottle of pills. "She doesn't have anything in here that would be medicine. Maybe we should call her Uncle."

Tara grabbed for the purse like a drunk trying to hold onto thin air. "Purse . . . hand me."

Flynn yanked the purse out of Nikki's hand and plopped it in Tara's lap, then put her hand on it.

"Here it is. Show me. Show me. What do you need?"

Tara's head lolled forward. She felt boneless, but she could see her purse. She thrust her hand into the depths, and began to fumble through it. When she finally felt a chain between her fingers, she felt a surge of power through her body. She curled her hand around the chain and pulled it out.

"This . . . this . . ."

Flynn frowned. "A necklace? You wanted a necklace? That doesn't make sense."

Tara blinked. "On me . . ."

"Okay." Flynn tried twice to fasten the tiny clasp before Nikki pushed him aside.

"Let me," she said, and did it for him.

Within moments, Tara felt the energy within her beginning to change. Thoughts that had been bouncing between her ears like ping-pong balls gathered, and her body began to regain a sense of normalcy.

"Oh my God," she groaned, as she reached up and clasped the tiny pendant on the chain like a drowning man clutching at a life raft. As expected, it felt warm in her hand.

"What on earth?" Nikki asked.

Flynn crouched down beside Tara. She knew he could see the color come back into her face and her breathing return to normal.

Tara began to pull herself together. Slowly, she sat upright in the car, looking around in stunned confusion. "What happened? How did I get outside?"

Flynn shivered. "Girl, you are so out of it. You told me to take you out. Corey and Nikki came along and helped. Now tell me what the hell just happened to you?"

Tara shuddered, then swiped a hand across her face. "What did I say?"

Flynn's didn't mince words. "That someone wants you dead."

"Crap," Tara said.

"Crap that you said it, or crap that it's true?" Flynn asked.

"Both," Tara said, then looked at Corey and Nikki, aware that they'd accidentally become part of something she'd rather not be sharing. There was no way to explain without telling them the truth.

"What just happened to you?" Flynn asked again.

She angled a glance up at the other couple, then sighed. "So remember I'm sort of . . . sensitive, right?"

"I know you're sort of psychic," Corey said.

Tara's eyes widened as she looked up at him.

"You forget how we met? I haven't," Corey said.

Tara sighed. "Oh yeah. That."

Flynn frowned. "I don't get it."

Nikki elbowed Corey. "Tell him what you told me the day you got sick at school."

"You mean the day I died?"

Nikki nodded.

The expression on Flynn's face stilled. "For real, dude?"

"Yeah," Corey said. "For real. That day at school I remember feeling sick and going into the boys bathroom, then everything went black. The doctors said I had a seizure of some kind, then my heart stopped. The next thing I know, I'm still in the boys bathroom, but Coach Jones and a couple of teachers are down on the floor giving me CPR. Only I'm standing outside my body watching this happen and realize I'm standing beside this tall dark-haired girl I've never seen before.

"And she can see me. Talk about freaking . . . So I ask her. Am I dead? She tells me she thinks so. I tell her, I don't want to die. So she says, then go back. So I did. The next thing I know, my chest is killing me because Coach is pushing on it with all his two-hundred plus pounds, and someone else has my nose pinched shut and their mouth over my lips. I'm talking huge UGH factor here. Then the ambulance comes and off I go. I remember seeing you." He pointed at Tara. "You're the only person I can truly say that I've met twice. Once dead. Once alive."

Tara sighed. "I didn't know you remembered all that."

"How could I forget it?" Corey said. "You are such a lunatic."

"So I've been told," Tara said.

Flynn shook his head. "Okay. That's one for the books. You're one lucky dude."

Corey slid an arm around Nikki's shoulders. "I know. In more ways than one."

Nikki's green eyes twinkled, but she kept quiet.

Flynn pointed to the necklace around Tara's neck. "Exactly what was wrong with you, Moon girl, and why did that help you feel better?"

"I don't know where they're coming from, but I've been feeling some really ugly emotions. I didn't think much of it before, because I didn't think it was directed at me. Only now I'm not so sure. These emotions are so dark they make me physically sick. It's like my bones turn to mush and I can't think."

"The necklace," Flynn prodded. "What's that got to do with anything?"

Tara fingered the pendant, then turned it over.

Corey pointed. "Hey, I know what that is. It's a Saint Benedict medal, right?"

Tara nodded.

"One of the priests at my church has one. Are you Catholic, Tara?"

"No."

Flynn was still frowning. "What does religion have to do with the necklace, and how does that—"

Suddenly, Corey gasped. "Oh. Wow. I know. Something I remembered from catechism classes."

Tara sighed and slipped it beneath her shirt.

Flynn was losing patience. "Well?"

"Sometimes I wear it for protection," Tara said.

Flynn frowned. "Protection from what, damn it? And what do priests have to do with anything?"

"I think the St. Benedict medal is sometimes used as part of an exorcism," Corey said.

Flynn rocked back on his heels and then stood abruptly. "As in demons and evil?"

He stared down at Tara. "Are you—"

"No, no, nothing like that," Tara said. "At least I don't think it's anything like that. People can be evil, and when they are, I feel it. This helps shield me from bad spirits, whether they're alive or dead."

"Thank God," Flynn mumbled.

Nikki was watching Tara's face and seemed to realize she wasn't telling everything she knew. "Are you sure you're okay?"

Tara nodded. "Thanks to both of you for helping Flynn drag me out before I made total fools of the both of us."

Flynn frowned. "You need to stop worrying so much about what everyone else thinks about you, Moon girl, and concentrate on keeping yourself in one piece." Then he glanced down at his watch. "It's almost midnight. I'm taking you home."

"Yes, we were about to do the same," Nikki said. "Dad is on a tear because the phone bill is too high. He said it's because I sent too many texts this month. And it's so not true." Then she grinned. "At least, I don't think so. Anyway, I don't want him angry at me over something else, too."

Then she leaned into Flynn's car and gave Tara a hug. "Take care of yourself, lunatic. I've sort of gotten attached to your goofy face."

Tara was stunned by the show of affection. After what had happened, she wouldn't have blamed them if they'd never wanted to be around her again. Her life was insane.

"Thanks for the help," she said, and began buckling up as Flynn circled the car and slid behind the wheel.

"I'm so sorry," she said softly. "We were having so much fun, and I feel like I've ruined the whole evening."

Flynn stared at her a moment, as if trying to figure out how to put into words what he was feeling. Finally, he just shook his head.

"You scared me, big time, but nothing was ruined. Except for what just happened, tonight has been one of the best times I've had in forever."

Tara sighed, then flashed a grateful smile. "Me, too."

He grinned, and then winked. "That's what a guy wants to

hear. Now I'd better get you home before you turn into a pumpkin."

"Hey. Cinderella didn't turn into the pumpkin. It was the coach she was riding in that turned into the pumpkin."

"I know, but you're not much for sticking to the rules, are you?"

"I see your point," she said, and then grinned. "So, we'd better hurry before the clock strikes midnight."

Flynn started the car and began to back out of the parking place. He didn't know, and Tara wasn't about to tell him, that Henry was riding in the back seat with them. She kept feeling him touching the back of her neck and the top of her hair, as if wanting her to know he was nearby. Obviously, whatever had happened to her was enough to get both Henry and Millicent upset. She wished she knew what or who was sending her such bad vibes.

By the time Flynn pulled into the driveway, Henry was gone and Tara was feeling fine and wondering if he was going to kiss her goodnight.

Trying to second guess a romantic moment was freaky.

"Looks like Mom and your Uncle Pat are still out. I don't see your car."

"Yeah," Tara said.

"Will you be all right by yourself?" Flynn asked. "I don't mind waiting around with you until he comes back."

"I'll be fine," Tara said.

Flynn frowned. "But what if you . . . uh, if that feeling . . . "

"You mean what if I freak out again?"

"That's not what I said," Flynn said.

"Don't worry," Tara said, and pulled the St. Benedict medal out from beneath her shirt. "I'm wired, remember."

Flynn just shook his head. "You are such a nut. But my favorite nut, just the same."

Tara grinned as Flynn got out and came around the car to walk her to the door. Thank goodness he was cool about what had happened. Once on the porch, she unlocked the front door. When she turned around to tell Flynn goodnight, he put his arms around her waist and pulled her close.

I am so falling for you, Tara thought, as she slipped her arms around his neck and leaned into his kiss.

The touch of his mouth on her lips was scary, scary good. Tara tingled all over, from her head to her toes, and when he kissed her again, she shuddered on a sigh.

Finally, Flynn groaned and pulled back. "You could become an addiction, Moon girl," he said softly.

Tara shivered at such sweet words from a sweet guy. "Don't quit on me, Flynn. I know of a good twelve-step program."

He chuckled beneath his breath. "You don't have anything to worry about. I'm not a quitter."

"Neither am I," Tara said, then opened the door and flipped on the inside light.

"I'm bussing tables tomorrow at Joe's, so, I'll see you Monday at school."

"Absolutely."

He touched the end of her nose with his finger. "Try to stay out of trouble, okay?"

"I'll do what I can," Tara said, practically buzzing with subdued joy as she watched him walk back to the car.

"I'm not leaving until you're locked inside the house," Flynn called.

Tara waved, then slipped inside and quickly locked herself in.

Flynn honked once, and then he was gone.

Tara wrapped her arms around herself and gazed around the room. Everything looked fine—just the way they'd left it. So why did she still have such an uneasy feeling?

Just to be on the safe side, she walked through all the rooms, checking to make sure the windows were locked and the curtains were drawn. Then she went into the kitchen and got a cold Dr. Pepper out of the fridge. She was digging through the pantry for something to go with it when she heard a key in the front door.

Thank goodness. Uncle Pat was home.

"I'm in the kitchen," she yelled.

"Save me some cookies," he called back.

She grinned and pulled the cookie jar off the shelf and carried it to the table as her uncle entered the kitchen. From the smile on his face, he'd had a good night, too.

"Have fun?" she asked, as he dug into the cookie jar and pulled out a handful of chocolate sandwich cookies.

"Yeah. We ate dinner at Red Lobster and then went to see a movie with that Downey guy. Iron Man II."

"Oh. Yeah. Was it good?" Tara asked, as she pulled her sandwich cookie apart and began licking off the icing.

"Why do you always do that?" Pat frowned, pointing at her cookie.

"I don't know. Makes them last longer, I guess."

"Yes, the movie was good," he said, then went to the fridge and got out a cold pop and sat down at the table with Tara.

"So. What did you and Flynn do?" he asked.

"Ate pizza at The Hideaway. We *have* to go there together some time. It's the best pizza I ever ate."

"Even better than Chicago deep dish?"

"Way better."

"Better than New York City pies?"

"Oh yeah," Tara said.

Pat just shook his head. "I find that hard to believe. You're right. We'll have to give it a try one of these days. So, what did you do afterwards?"

"We went bowling. There's this cool bowling alley called Frontier Lanes out toward Boomer Lake. Nice place. And you know me. I got beat royally."

Pat grinned. "No one's perfect."

Tara nodded, refusing to elaborate on the night. He didn't need to know about the toddler who'd choked at the restaurant, or the fact that she'd freaked out at the bowling alley. There were some things that were better left unsaid.

She reached for another cookie. "This one is my last then I'm headed to bed."

"What's on the docket for tomorrow? Do you have any

plans?" Pat asked.

"A little homework. Nothing big."

"I thought I'd plant that mum bed tomorrow. I bought the mums earlier this evening. They're in the garage."

"If you don't start the project at eight a.m., I might be persuaded to help."

Her uncle grinned and shrugged. "Not making any promises," he said, as he chewed and swallowed his last cookie. "Dibs on the bathroom first. I won't be long."

"Night, Uncle Pat," Tara said.

"Night, kiddo," he said, then added, "See you later alligator."

Tara grinned. "After while crocodile."

Uncle Pat was so goofy.

Tara was standing on the back porch, *watching a tall, broad-shouldered man dig a hole in the far corner of the backyard. He was knee-deep in the hole, throwing shovel after shovel full of dirt over his shoulder onto a nearby pile. Moonlight glinted every now and then on the metal part of the spade while an owl hooted from a nearby tree.*

She felt the tension in his body as he paused from time to time to wipe the sweat from his brow. A tomcat squalled from the alley nearby, which set a couple of dogs to barking. She saw the man stop, tilting his head as he listened. When he was satisfied he was still alone, he resumed digging.

She kept thinking she needed to walk out to where he was and ask him what he was doing, but she couldn't get off the porch. She tried to call out, to ask him what had he done with Uncle Pat, but when she opened her mouth, no sound came out.

All of a sudden, he stopped and climbed out of the hole. He stabbed the shovel into the dirt pile, then headed to the house. Now Tara wanted to run, but once again, she couldn't move.

When he got close enough that she could see his face, she didn't recognize him, at first. Then it hit her. She was looking at a younger version of Emmit Broyles. Now the need to run was overwhelming. What would he do when he found her on the porch?

To her shock, he walked right past her as if she wasn't even there. A few moments later, he came out of the house with an oblong bundle thrown over his shoulder. As he passed her again, she noticed something was dripping out of one end of the bundle, something that looked like ink droplets. It wasn't until he stepped off the porch and the bundle bumped against his back that the folds parted and she saw a human arm flop out.

OMG. OMG. Was that DeeDee? Were those ink droplets really blood? Why couldn't she move? Was this a nightmare, or was she seeing into the past?

The man carried the bundle all the way across the yard. When he reached the hole he'd dug, he paused.

Tara held her breath.

He leaned forward, shifting the weight of the bundle from his shoulder to his arm. Then he straddled the hole and without hesitation, dropped it in.

Tara's scream was silent. She had just witnessed DeeDee Broyles' burial.

The first thing Tara heard when she woke up was rain running off the roof. She rolled over with a groan, glanced at the digital clock on the end table by her bed, and groaned again. Ten minutes after nine. She sniffed the air, knowing that she would be smelling coffee if Uncle Pat was up.

Nothing.

She swiped her hands across her face and when she looked up, DeeDee was standing beside her bed.

"Yikes!" Tara squealed, and then flinched when DeeDee spun up and into the corner of the room. "Sorry," she said. "You startled me."

Tara could feel the little ghost's intensity. She knew why she'd come and what she wanted to hear.

"Yes, I got the message," Tara said, remembering the dream in detail. "I don't know who killed you for sure, but I do know who buried you. Emmit, right?"

DeeDee spun into a dark, angry shadow and flew across the ceiling.

"Don't be angry," Tara said. "I'm going to make this right.

I promise."

Tara felt the little ghost's energy shift from anger to sadness.

"Just give me a little time. I don't want to ruin what will ultimately become a crime scene by digging around on my own. I have to figure out how to make these two detectives I know believe there's a body buried somewhere out near the fence without having any proof that it's there."

DeeDee disappeared.

The burden of proof was now upon Tara. Somewhere between studying for a Spanish test and writing a paper on Captain Ahab's motivation in *Moby Dick*, she had to solve a really old murder case.

Piece of cake.

And speaking of cake, she was going to see if there was any left of the bakery cake Uncle Pat had brought home from the supermarket. Nothing like a healthy breakfast of carrot cake with cream cheese icing and a glass of milk.

She dressed in shorts and a clean tee and headed for the kitchen, her bare feet making little splat, splat sounds on the old hardwood floors. A rumble of distant thunder rolled through the air.

Henry sailed down the hall, passing Tara on the left.

"I know, I know. You don't like thunder, right?"

Henry shifted from ghost to ectoplasm and disappeared.

He's entirely too sensitive.

"Now, Millicent. You know Henry doesn't like storms."

They displace his energy.

"I know. Henry doesn't like to be displaced." Tara opened the refrigerator where she saw the bakery box with the carrot cake on the bottom shelf. "Score!"

I always favored chocolate.

Tara pulled out the box, then the jug of milk. "Yum," she said, as she cut a piece of cake and poured milk in her glass. Then she scooted into a chair at the table and took her first bite. "Double yum."

How rude.

Tara heard a soft pop, then Millicent was gone. She was putting her dirty dishes in the dishwasher when she heard her uncle's footsteps coming down the hall.

"Morning, Uncle Pat," she said, as he walked into the kitchen.

His steps were slow and his eyes were red-rimmed and watery. When he walked past her and went to the cabinet where he kept his whiskey, she frowned, then looked away. It was times like this that she wished she was older. She didn't know what to do or say to him now.

"How long has it been raining?" he asked.

"I don't know. It was raining when I woke up."

He poured a shot of whiskey into a juice glass, then filled it the rest of the way up with juice. "This weather definitely puts a kink into my plan to plant the mums." He downed the juice like medicine, in one gulp.

"Maybe it will pass later on," Tara said.

"Yeah. Maybe. Have you eaten?"

"Yep. Cake and milk."

"Not exactly a balanced breakfast," he said, as he started the coffee pot.

And neither was the shot of whiskey, Tara thought, but didn't say it. "*Au contraire,*" Tara said. "The cake had eggs, a good source of protein. Butter, a necessary oil. Flour in lieu of bread. Carrots from the vegetable menu. Crushed pineapple from the fruit section. And milk, which is dairy. A perfectly balanced meal."

He laughed. "If you ignore all the sugar. So, how about we eat out at noon?"

Tara was relieved the awkwardness of the moment had passed. "Got a place in mind?"

"Want to try Mexico Joe's? It's owned by the same guy who runs Eskimo Joe's. I've been hungry for fajitas."

"Oooh, good choice. Remember what good ones we used to get at Ninfa's?"

Pat smiled. "Ah. Houston. I liked it there."

"That was where I got chicken-pox," Tara said. "Talk

about miserable."

Pat slid his arm around her shoulders and gave her a hug. "I've put you through a lot, haven't I, honey?"

Tara shrugged. "I admit I don't love moving like you do, but I love you, Uncle Pat, and wherever you go, I go."

Pat shook his head, and then pulled her into his arms and hugged her again.

"Love you, little girl."

"Love you, back, Uncle Pat," Tara said softly.

Chapter Four

Tara was downing her third tortilla-wrapped chicken fajita when the skin suddenly crawled on the back of her neck. Without making a fuss, she looked up, sweeping the area with a steady gaze. There was a young man she didn't know sitting in the booth beside her.

Tara jumped. It wasn't as if she'd never seen a ghost before, but they didn't always pop up right in her lap. It was obvious he was trying to get her attention, but she had a fajita to chew and swallow and an uncle to consider, not to mention the other diners all over the restaurant.

I know you're here, she thought, *but give me a break. It's Sunday. Supposed to be a day of rest and all that stuff. Consider me off the clock, okay?*

Her spoon slid toward her elbow and dropped onto the floor.

"Oops." Tara looked up at her uncle. "Clumsy me."

She bent over to pick it up, and as she did, found herself eye to eye with the persistent spirit.

"What?" she hissed.

Tell my mother I didn't commit suicide. Tell her it was an accident.

"You okay down there?" Uncle Pat asked Tara.

"Yep. Just fine." She straightened back up and laid the spoon on the table.

At that point, Uncle Pat's phone began to ring. He glanced down at caller ID, then grinned sheepishly. "It's Mona. I'll take it outside. Be right back."

"Okay," Tara said. Mona's timing couldn't be better. The moment her uncle was gone, she focused on the spirit. "I don't know your Mother," Tara said. "And even if I did, I can't just go up and tell her something like that."

She's sitting at that back booth. She's the one with the red blouse and sad face.

"Rats," Tara muttered, then turned to look over her shoulder. Sure enough, there was a small, slim woman with short brown hair sitting all alone in the back booth.

She's waiting for my sister. Please. While she's still by herself.

"You don't understand," Tara whispered. Then she took a bite of fajita hoping that chewing would mask the fact that she was talking to herself. "Saying it doesn't make it so. I have no proof."

I fell asleep at the wheel in broad daylight the morning after I broke up with my girlfriend. Everyone thought I drove into that tree on purpose, but I didn't. Tell her to call a man named Dr. Ira Pershing in Oklahoma City. He'll confirm I was being treated for sleep apnea.

Tara sighed. "I don't even know your name."

David Morris, but everyone called me Butch.

"What's your mother's name?"

Sherry Morris.

Tara groaned, then took a sip of iced tea, wiped her mouth with a napkin, and grabbed her purse just as Pat came back to the table.

"Everything okay with Mona?" she asked.

He nodded. "She wants me to come over tonight. Said Flynn had to work, but she didn't. We could watch a movie together at the house. I told her I'd see."

Tara rolled her eyes. "Call her back and say yes. I'm not a baby. I do not need a sitter."

He grinned sheepishly.

"Uh, Uncle Pat, I see a friend I want to say hi to," Tara said. "Hold down the fort."

Pat nodded, already in the act of calling Mona as Tara left the table.

The moment Tara started toward the table where Sherry Morris was sitting, she could feel her sadness. She didn't know how this was going to play out, but she knew from experience that the fastest way to get rid of a troubled spirit was to help them.

Without hesitation, she slid into the booth where David's mother was sitting.

"Excuse me," Tara said softly. "I know this is rude of me, but aren't you Butch Morris's mother?"

Tara flinched as she saw shock and then sadness pass over the woman's face.

"Yes, I am," Sherry Morris said. "Did you know my son?"

"Yes, I met him once," Tara said. "I just wanted to say how sorry I was for what happened."

Sherry nodded, but her lips were pressed together so tightly that they were white, and Tara could see her body physically shaking. Here was where it got tricky.

She slid her hand over Sherry's hand. "You know Butch didn't kill himself, don't you?"

Huge tears welled and spilled over Sherry Morris's cheeks. "I don't want to talk about this," she said. "Please. You have to go now."

Tara sighed. "I know what I'm talking about. Butch wanted me to tell you that he'd been diagnosed with sleep apnea, but hadn't told anyone. I don't know why."

Sherry gasped, then suddenly she was the one holding on to Tara. "He wanted to fly. For as long as I can remember, the only thing he ever wanted to be was a pilot. He'd been taking lessons for over six months."

"Ah," Tara said, suddenly understanding why David Morris wouldn't have told. "People who fly planes can't have sleep apnea, can they?"

"No. No, they can't," Sherry said. "Dear Lord, dear Lord, are you sure?"

"He said to tell you to call a Doctor Ira Pershing in Oklahoma City. He could confirm this."

Sherry Morris started to shake. "You're sure? You wouldn't lie to me about this, would you?"

"No, ma'am."

Tears were still flowing, but there was a light behind them, as if a terrible burden had been lifted.

"What I don't understand is why would Butch tell you and

not his family? Were you two dating?"

"No, ma'am. I never met Butch . . . when he was alive."
Then Tara stood. "He's okay, Mrs. Morris. He just wanted you
to know the truth."

Tara started to walk away when Sherry stopped her with a
cry. "Wait! Please!"

Here it comes. She sighed, then turned around. "Yes,
ma'am?"

"What do you mean you never met him when he was alive?
How else would you have known to tell me?"

Tara didn't answer. Instead, she watched comprehension
dawning on Sherry Morris's face as the silence lengthened.

"Oh. I don't believe . . . Oh my God. Can you really . . . ?
Dear Lord . . . is he—"

"Standing behind you," Tara said softly. "He wouldn't
cross over until you knew the truth. Tell him goodbye, Mrs.
Morris. He's been waiting for you to tell him goodbye."

Tara turned around and walked back to the table. Her eyes
were brimming with tears, but in a good way.

"Did you eat that last tortilla?" Tara asked, as she slid into
her seat.

Pat Carmichael looked guilty, then nodded. "I'll get more."

Tara eyed the icky remnants of the congealing grease on
the chicken and peppers and then shook her head. "No thanks.
I'll settle for some ice cream, later."

"Deal," Pat said, then noticed Tara's teary expression. "Is
everything all right?"

Tara blinked, as if surprised by the question. "Yes. Why?"

"You look like you've been crying."

She rolled her eyes. "Oh. That. Yeah, uh, my friend
accidentally squirted lemon juice in my eyes. It's almost quit
burning."

"Ouch," Pat said. "You sure you don't need to go to the
ladies room to wash it out?"

"No. I'm fine. I'm ready to go when you are."

"Then home it is," her uncle said.

Tara looked back once toward Sherry Morris's table as they

were walking out the door. Her daughter had joined her and they were head to head, talking a mile a minute. Just as she looked, she saw a bright flash of light and then a pop. David Morris's spirit had finally crossed.

Safe travels, Butch, she thought.

Monday was Career Day at school. Recruiting officers from different branches of the Armed Forces elicited serious, thoughtful looks from students who were well aware that joining a branch of the armed forces meant going to war. Detectives Rutherford and Allen, from the Stillwater Police Department, who Tara had met when Bethany had been kidnapped, were on hand representing law enforcement. There was a father who was a long-haul trucker, a beautician from one of the local beauty shops, and several professors from Oklahoma State University who were pushing higher education in their chosen fields.

Tara listened with interest and a little bit of fear. The future was an unknown, and unknowns were always uncomfortable, especially when her only natural skills involved seeing ghosts. She knew she was going to have to find something worthwhile—something interesting—that would become her career.

So when she walked into third hour and found a pair of men standing near the teacher's desk, she slid into her seat with a feeling of anticipation, wondering what they had to offer that she hadn't already seen.

When class began, the teacher introduced the first man, who turned out to be a lawyer, Tara wondered if Flynn had heard him yet. She knew he was interested in getting into law or law enforcement. She listened politely, but she didn't think law was the field for her. It would be too frustrating to always know the truth behind a crime or a trial and not be able to prove it.

The second young man, Nate Pierce, turned out to be an assistant professor in the geology department at OSU. She wasn't sure she her career path included geology, but Tara realized he might have other information she needed. He spoke for about ten minutes and then took questions. Tara held up her hand when he'd finished answering the last one.

"Yes, miss?" the professor asked.

The moment Nate Pierce looked into Tara's eyes, she got a flash of sadness so deep she wanted to cry. It took her aback so much she actually choked on her first word, which made everyone laugh. That gave her the moment she needed to get herself together.

"Sorry," Tara said. "Nothing like choking on your own spit."

That brought another round of laughter, and to her surprise, she felt a lightening of Nate Pierce's sadness. She sighed. No biggy making a fool of yourself if it changes that kind of grief.

"Okay, as I was trying to say earlier," Tara said, "you were talking about Ground Penetrating Radar and how cool it was that you could, in effect, 'see what was underground' sort of like an x-ray machine seeing the bones inside our bodies."

"Yes?"

"So here's my question. Exactly what does it show?"

Nate frowned. "I'm not sure what you're asking."

Tara bit her lip. Here's where it might get tricky. "Um, is it ever used outside of the geological field? For instance, I was watching a documentary on TV not too long ago about a serial killer, and the film clip had to do with trying to find the bodies of the victims the killer had buried. What I'm asking is . . . can you see bodies—actual bodies? Could it be used for something like that?"

"It's not exactly like x-rays in that aspect, but the GPR will show if the earth below has ever been disturbed. Here's what I mean. You know the earth is in layers, right?"

Tara nodded.

"Okay. Picture this. Someone made a three-layer cake. Before they could take it to the party, something fell on it, messing part of it up. So the baker put everything back together as best he could. He pushed everything back where it belonged, put a fresh layer of icing on it, and on the outside, it looks good as new, right?"

"Right," she echoed.

"But when it's cut, it will be obvious that the original cake had been damaged because the layers are not in alignment. Understand?"

"Yes. Yes. So, if anyone had *ever* dug a hole, like to plant a big tree, or lay foundation for a house that's no longer there, or even a grave, you could see that place. You might not know what the displacement had been for, but you could tell where the displacement had happened and the shape of it, right?"

He grinned, and Tara felt his genuine delight, which she knew came from being a teacher who'd shared knowledge with a student who got it.

"Right!" he said.

"One last question," Tara asked.

"Yes?"

"Does the OSU geology department have GPR?"

"Yes."

"Cool," she said. "Thanks."

A few minutes later, the session was over. Then the bell rang, signaling the end of class. The teacher was thanking the career day speakers as students filed out of class. As Tara passed by, she caught Nate Pierce watching her.

She smiled quickly, then walked away. Professor Pierce didn't know it, but he hadn't seen the last of her.

Beyoncé was playing on Tara's iPod as she walked home from school. She'd said goodbye to Flynn at the schoolyard. He had a test to study for, and she was on a mission. For the time being, she was keeping her plan to herself. And, before she went home, Tara was stopping by the Geology department on the OSU campus. She wasn't sure how she was going to make it happen, but now that she had a way to find the location of DeeDee Broyles' grave, she wasn't passing up the opportunity.

Living on Duck Street made her trip to the campus easy, since Duck Street bordered parts of it on the east. She'd used one of the computers at school to get a map of the campus. As soon as she reached the intersection of Duck Street and Miller Avenue, she headed west on Miller toward the geology building.

Students were thick on the sidewalks, which meant classes were changing. Tara knew she was taking a chance on catching Nate Pierce in his office, but she was too far along now to chicken out.

She met and then passed a trio of young men who eyed her appreciatively, but she kept on walking. She had enough on her plate without all that. Besides, she had Flynn. A short while later she'd reached the Noble Research Center where the Boone Pickens School of Geology was located. She'd found the building. Now all she needed was to find the man.

She braced herself and went inside, asked the first person she met where Nate Pierce's office was located and was directed up to the second floor. She took the stairs before she chickened out. A couple of minutes later, she'd located his office.

"Please let him be there," she said, as she started to knock.

Yep. He's there, and he's cute.

Tara flinched. Just when she thought she'd snuck around and done something on her own. She should have known you can't escape someone you can't see. *Millicent! Do not, and I mean it, do not mess this up. It's important. I'm trying to help DeeDee, okay?*

I was simply passing along pertinent information.

Fine. So was I.

Whatever.

Tara frowned, then knocked. She heard a faint voice telling her to come in.

Nate Pierce was at the desk with a stack of papers on his left and a smaller stack on his right. The red pen he was holding left Tara with the impression he was grading papers. His thick black hair gleamed from the sunlight coming through the window behind him. His shoulders were broad beneath his blue denim shirt, and his warm brown skin and high cheekbones highlighted his Native American heritage.

Tara eyed him nervously. When he didn't look up, she loudly cleared her throat.

He paused, and glanced up. "Yes?" Then he frowned. "You aren't one of my students."

"No, I'm not."

"Wait. Aren't you the girl from third hour Career Day with the interesting questions?"

"Yes. My name is Tara Luna."

She saw him sigh, then bite the inside of his jaw. Obviously, this was not a good time.

"I'm sorry to bother you like this, but I have a very important question to ask you."

To her relief, he managed a sideways grin. "It wouldn't happen to have anything more to do with GPR would it?"

"Yes, actually it does."

"So ask," he said.

"I want to know if you would bring that GPR to my house. Specifically, the back yard of my house, and map it?"

Startled, he leaned back, his eyes wide with surprise. "First of all, it's not a toy, and it's not for personal use, which means the answer is no."

"I'm well aware it's not a toy. And it wouldn't be for me. It would be a service for the Stillwater Police Department."

Now she had his attention. "What on earth could possibly be buried in your back yard that would interest the police? And even more to the point, why aren't they asking?"

Tara sighed. Just once, couldn't this be easy? "Well, it's like this. There's a body buried somewhere in the backyard. It's been there for more than twenty years, and the police don't know it. Yet. I need you to find where it is before I confront them."

Nate stood up with a jerk as his chair went rolling backwards, hitting the row of file cabinets with a thunk. "Are you serious?"

"Yes."

"What makes you think there's a body in your back yard? Is some of your family involved in this?"

"Oh, no. Uncle Pat and I only moved here from Denver right before school started. We're renting it from Mr. Whiteside, who owns it. It's not far. Just down Duck Street."

"Listen, Tara. I don't know what kind of a joke you're trying to pull. If you're into punking people or whatever, but I'm busy and you need to leave."

Tara squinted her eyes and concentrated on his face. Within moments, she flashed on a young woman and a baby, then a wreck, then flowers on the ground. All of a sudden, she knew the source of Nate Pierce's sadness. His wife and baby had been killed in a car wreck.

"It's not a joke. I'm serious. And I know it's there because the ghost of the woman who was buried there still haunts the house. Her name is . . . I mean, her name was DeeDee Broyles, and I promised her I'd find her body, which would start the investigation into her death. She doesn't know who killed her, but I think I do. I think it was her brother, Emmit, although he denies even having a sister, and—"

Nate circled the desk and then put his finger so close to her nose it made her cross-eyed. "Shut up," he said softly. "Just shut up. I don't want to hear any more of this BS. I don't know what you're trying to pull, but I do not for a minute think you can talk to ghosts, and I'm not taking the GPR to your house and winding up pranked and on YouTube."

"Sometimes you smell lilacs in your bathroom, even though you threw out all your wife's shampoos and soaps after her funeral. It's her. She's just telling you she sees you."

He held up his hands and walked backwards, obviously wanting to get as far away from her as possible.

"You do not talk about my wife. Ever. Get out. Now."

Tara felt like crying. "I wish I could," she said. "But I made a promise to DeeDee and I need you to make it happen."

"Do you have parents? Are you on drugs? You have freaking lost your mind if you think I'm going to believe a damn thing you're saying."

Tara dropped into a chair and then crossed her arms and glared. "You stole a Baby Ruth candy bar from a drug store in Muskogee, Oklahoma when you were nine years old. Your grandfather caught you, made you take it back and apologize."

All the color faded from Nate's face as he stared at Tara in disbelief. "How did you know that?" he whispered. "Granddad never told my folks, and neither did I."

"I'm psychic. It's not something I'm particularly happy about, but it's how I came into the world. Do you want more proof? Okay. How about this. The first girl you ever did it with was Sonya Friend. She was sixteen and you were fourteen." Tara pointed at him. "And don't deny it."

His face turned red as a beet, but she had his attention. "Okay. Answer this and I might be willing to consider your request."

"What's the question?" Tara asked.

"I have a cousin named Jimmy who's been missing for almost two years. If you can—"

"He's in prison."

Nate inhaled sharply, then eased himself down onto the corner of his desk.

"How do you know that?"

"Haven't you been listening to me? I'm psychic, okay?"

"Where? Which prison? His mother, my Aunt Jean, thinks he's dead. She's been in a serious state of depression for over a year."

"Well, tell her to write to him in care of McAlester State Penitentiary. He'll write back. He was just too ashamed to let anyone know."

Nate pointed at her. "Don't move," he said softly, then grabbed his phone and within moments, found the number to the prison and made a call.

Tara crossed her legs and leaned back, watching the changing expressions on his face. For an old guy, he was pretty hot. She guessed he was at least twenty-six or twenty-seven, but he had good hair. She eyed his changing expressions as she waited for his call to go through. Then she saw him sat up a little straighter and reach for a pen.

"Yes. My name is Nate Pierce. I'm an Assistant Professor at Oklahoma State University, and just recently learned a family member, who's been missing for over two years, is possibly an inmate there. How do I go about confirming that?"

"Just give them his name," Tara muttered.

"Oh. His name?"

Tar rolled her eyes. "Told you," she added beneath her breath, at which point, he looked at her and glared. She shrugged as he answered.

"His name is James Lee Pierce. He's twenty-two years old. Native American descent. Choctaw tribe."

Tara smirked. She already knew that, thank you very much.

"Yes, thank you. I'll wait."

Nate put his hand over the mouthpiece and looked at Tara. "Smart ass comments are not appreciated," he said, then his focus shifted. "Yes, I'm here."

Tara watched his eyes widen, then his attention shift back to her.

"He's there," Nate repeated. "He's been there almost seventeen months. Good Lord. His mother thinks he's dead. Wait. Wait. I need visiting days . . . hours, whatever a family needs to know to make a visit."

He was writing quickly, taking down everything he was being told.

"One more thing," Nate asked. "How long before he comes up for parole?"

"Nine more months," Tara said.

Nate pointed at her again, as if warning her to stay quiet, then his mouth dropped.

"Okay. Nine months, you said?"

Tara smirked.

"Thank you very much," Nate said, then very slowly hung up the phone.

"He's there."

Tara rolled her eyes. "Oh my God. Did I just not say that

already?"

"But . . ."

"The GPR?"

Nate stood up. "I owe you big time," he said. "I'll let the Dean know that I'm taking it out."

"When?" Tara asked.

Nate glanced at the unmarked papers on his desk, then the daily planner on his desk.

"I have classes tomorrow until three."

"I get out of school about the same time. My place tomorrow afternoon. Four o'clock."

Nate shoved his hands in his pockets. "You're scary. You know that, don't you?"

"Why? Because I can see and talk to ghosts? Because I know things about people?"

"I have to be losing my mind to agree to this," Nate muttered.

"Just think of it as an extension of Career Day."

"I will never volunteer to do that again," he said.

"Okay. So. I think we're done here," Tara said.

"No. We're not," Nate said. "Unlike you, I am not psychic, so I need your address."

Tara grinned. "Oh. Yeah. Right." She leaned across the desk and scribbled her name, phone number, and address on his daily planner. "Just in case you're inclined to forget."

"Oh. I'm not likely to forget this conversation," he drawled.

"Good. DeeDee and I both thank you," she said. "See you tomorrow."

Tara grabbed her backpack, slung it over one shoulder and strode out of his office without looking back.

Before she reached the end of the hallway, she heard Nate's voice again. "Hey! Mom! It's me, Nate. Oh, yeah, I'm fine. Grading papers. But the reason I called . . . you will not guess. I found Jimmy. I'm serious. Yes, he's alive. No. I'm not calling Aunt Pam. She'll just cry and I don't want to hear her cry. That's why I called you. You're going to be the one to break the news. So, get this . . . "

Chapter Five

Tara got home thirty minutes before her Uncle Pat. She spread her books all over the kitchen table so it would look like she'd been working, then got hamburger meat from the fridge and quickly made two patties and put them on to cook. Hamburgers and fries would put a smile on his face and fill his tummy at the same time.

I never did understand the concept of chopping up meat just to form it back into the same shape again.

Tara grinned, as she slid the skillet onto the stove. "You're so right, Millicent. It is weird, but I promise you, hamburgers are good."

I once had escargot in Paris. That was good.

"Eww. So wrong. Aren't those snails?"

Anything spoken in French tastes and sounds better. Oui?

"No thank you to snails in any language," Tara said.

She reached for the salt and pepper, doused the burgers liberally, and turned down the fire before getting a bag of frozen french fries out of the freezer. Within a few minutes, she had the fries in the oven and buns warming on the back of the stove. After slicing a tomato, laying out some lettuce and pickles, and peeling an onion, she turned the burger patties, then turned off the burner. They would finish cooking in the pan and still be warm when Uncle Pat arrived. She stirred the fries and turned off the oven, giving them the same treatment as the meat. He would be home by the time everything had finished cooking.

Supper was done. Satisfied, she slid into a chair and pulled her notebook forward. On to homework, but it was hard to concentrate. She kept thinking about tomorrow and Nate Pierce's arrival. This was going to start a brush fire of controversy, but it couldn't be helped. DeeDee deserved justice. Tara took a deep breath, savoring the aromas of the food, and hoped Uncle Pat got here soon. She was starving.

Less than fifteen minutes later she heard his key in the lock.

"I'm home!" Pat called.

"In the kitchen," Tara called back, and shoved her homework to the side as she got up.

Pat came striding into the kitchen with his lunch box under his arm and his cap in his hands.

"Something smells good," he said.

"Burgers and fries."

"Sounds great," Pat said, as he gave his niece a hug and a kiss on the cheek. "Have a good day, honey?"

"I guess. Nothing out of the ordinary."

"I thought today was Career Day."

"It was, but I didn't get any urges to follow anyone else's dreams." She frowned as she washed her hands at the kitchen sink. "I wish I knew what my dream is supposed to be."

"You have all kinds of time to worry about a career," Pat said. "I don't know about you, but I'm hungry."

"Me, too," Tara said. "I'll fix our plates while you go wash up."

"Back in a few. And since you cooked, I'll clean."

Tara grinned. "It's a deal."

When Tara turned around, Henry was floating above the table.

"What?"

He pointed toward the bathroom at the same time that Tara heard Uncle Pat yell.

"OMG! What's happening?" Tara cried.

It was just a case of too many bubbles.

"Millicent! You didn't!"

"Tara! What on earth, honey?" Pat yelled, as he bolted out of the bathroom. "There's water on the floor and the tub is full of bubbles. You must have forgotten to turn off the water."

Tara frowned. She could take the blame, but there was no

need now that Uncle Pat knew that she saw ghosts.

"I didn't do that," she said. "Millicent is the one with the bubble fetish. You yell at her a while, and I'll go get the mop."

The look on her uncle's face was priceless. "You're kidding."

"No. I'm not," Tara said, and if she wasn't going to have to mop up the floor, she might have laughed. As she walked away, she could hear her uncle trying to figure out how to chastise someone he couldn't see.

School was a drag, at least from the standpoint of time. All day, Tara kept picturing the moment when she and Nate would find DeeDee's grave. Even the classes she had with Flynn, who made everything fun, never seemed to end. By the time the bell rang to dismiss school, she was fired up like a roman candle on the Fourth of July. She bolted from her seat, made a quick stop at her locker, and slipped out a side door instead of taking the front, knowing full well she was going to miss seeing Flynn. She didn't have time to delay or explain, and she had a feeling he wouldn't be all that thrilled in what she was doing. He was pretty cool about her psychic stuff, but digging for bodies fell way out of the realm of normal—even for her.

She jogged out of the schoolyard, then down the street. By the time she turned the corner on Duck Street, she was running. To her relief, she beat Nate Pierce to her house by almost five minutes. Just enough time to put on her old shoes and snag a quick snack. She was eating her third chocolate chip cookie when someone knocked on the door.

"Yay!" She headed for the door on the run. "You came," Tara cried, as she opened the door.

"I didn't know I had an option," Nate said, as he stifled a sigh. "I've been dreading this all day, but a deal's a deal, and I'm a man of my word."

"Well, you know what I mean," Tara said, then caught movement from the corner of her eye and turned to look.

The small ghost floating near the hallway had obviously

caught wind of what was happening. Tara gave her a conspiratorial thumbs up and then handed the professor a couple of cookies. "Have some," she said. "They're pretty good. From the Wal-Mart bakery."

"I didn't come for tea. Let's just get this over with, okay?"

"Whatever." Tara took the cookies out of his hand and stuffed one in her mouth as she walked out on the porch with him. "So, there's a gate to the back yard on the north side of the house. Hope it's wide enough to get your radar through."

Looking regretfully at the cookies in her hand, Nate followed her off the porch, then got the GPR out of the back of a van belonging to the University Geology Department, and proceeded to the back yard.

"It's a big yard," he said.

"Is that a problem?" Tara asked.

"It will take longer than I thought."

Tara grinned and handed back one of the cookies. "There are more inside. Start with that one, and then lets's get started. I think we should start at the back side of the fence. I know it's not toward the house."

Nate frowned. "You know this how?"

"Um . . . DeeDee has been trying to show me in the only way she can, what happened. You know, if you don't see your killer coming at you from behind, you don't always know who did you in."

He just shook his head, put the cookie in his mouth, and headed to the back of the yard with the GPR, and Tara on his heels.

"It looks a little like a lawn mower with bicycle wheels and no blade underneath. Is all the stuff inside that flat black box-looking thingy?" she asked.

"Pretty much, except I'm hooking up what amounts to a laptop so we can see it as it scans." Nate said. "I'm going to start in the northwest corner. And you don't need to follow me."

But Tara was fascinated. "So if we find something that looks like it could be a grave, can this be printed out?"

"It can, but let's just worry about finding this grave of yours before we worry about anything else."

"Yes. Alright," Tara said.

A short while later, the process had begun. Tara could tell that the professor's patience was thin and his disbelief large. But she also knew that if this GPR gadget worked like it was supposed to, time would change that.

"I can't believe I'm doing this. Nobody at the university better find about it," Nate said. "By the way, my aunt is probably the only woman in the state who's ever been overjoyed to find out her son is in the pen. Er, um . . . thanks."

"Glad to help. And I appreciate your help, too," Tara said.

The process for mapping with a GPR was simple, really. Nate just wheeled it over the surface, in a pattern not unlike the paths one would make mowing a yard, while the radar read what lay below. With the laptop hooked up to it was possible to see the readouts as they occurred, rather than having to wait and look at print-outs later.

"What's that?" Tara asked, watching the computer screen over Nate's shoulder as they made pass after pass across the yard.

"It's not a grave, and that's all you need to know," Nate muttered.

Suddenly, DeeDee appeared at Tara's side. Tara felt her sadness all over again.

"We're trying," she said. "Just give us time."

"I'm sorry, what did you say?" Nate asked.

"Oh. I wasn't talking to you."

Nate paused. "Then who? If you hadn't noticed, we're alone out here. Do you talk to yourself often?"

"No, I do not talk to myself," Tara said, but to her regret, Nate wouldn't let it go.

"Then that begs the question, who are you talking to?"

"DeeDee. The ghost of the body you're looking for. She's here."

Nate's eyes widened as he glanced nervously around the yard. "I'm sorry I asked," he said, and resumed his sweep.

Tara sighed. All she'd done was give him even less reason to trust her, but it wasn't in her to lie just to assure Nate's comfort. Not after what she'd done in his office the day before.

A few moments later, someone else appeared in the yard, but it wasn't a ghost. It was Flynn, and when she looked up and saw him standing near the gate with a suspicious, almost angry look on his face, she figured she had some explaining to do.

"Hey!" she called, and waved him over. To her relief, he only hesitated briefly, before walking toward them. "It's my boyfriend," Tara said.

"God help him," Nate muttered.

Tara frowned. "That wasn't particularly nice."

"I'm not running for office."

"Really," Tara huffed and hurried to meet Flynn. "Hey." She threaded her fingers through his.

"Hey yourself," Flynn said, and then pointed at the professor. "Who's he and what's he doing?"

"That's Professor Pierce from the OSU Geology department."

"Okay, but what's he doing?" Flynn repeated.

"That's a little tricky."

"I have time," Flynn said, eyeing the tall, brown-skinned, broad-shouldered male in his girlfriend's backyard.

"He's using Ground Penetrating Radar, alias GPR, to help me find a body."

Flynn took a step backward. "Shut. Up."

Tara nodded. "I know. It sounds a little weird."

"You think?" Flynn watched the man make a sweep across the length of the yard. "Exactly whose body are you looking for, and why am I just hearing about this?"

Tara frowned. "Don't get all macho on me, mister. I don't tell you all my business just like you don't tell me yours. You don't hear me asking you where and what you're doing when I'm not around."

Flynn looked embarrassed, but he stood his ground.

"That's because you probably already know, being psychic and all."

Tara rolled her eyes. "OMG. Like all I have to do is worry about what you're doing when I have ghosts popping up around me on a daily basis? Get real! I haven't even told Uncle Pat, and he's higher up on my list of people I need to please than you are."

Flynn watched her carefully.

"We've already had one break-up over my psychic stuff. I'd really rather not have another one," she said.

"Okay. Okay. I'm sorry. Can we start this conversation over?"

Tara fixed him with a steady gaze. "You can try."

Flynn took a deep breath and started over. "So, how do you know there's a body buried in your backyard?" Then he swiped a hand over his face. "I can't believe I just asked that question."

Tara touched his arm. "I realize my life is a bit strange for the uninitiated, but I am who I am. So, here's the deal. There was a ghost in the house when we moved here. Without going into details about how I found out, I'll just tell you the high points. Her name is DeeDee Broyles. She and her family lived in this house. After her parents died, she and her brother, Emmit became joint owners. Only here's the rub. One day she was here and then she wasn't. Brother Emmit never reported her missing, and all of a sudden he was the sole owner of the property. And since no one knew she was missing, no one knew to look for her. Her body is buried somewhere in this yard. She doesn't know who killed her, or exactly where she's buried, because it was so long ago that the yard and everything around it has changed. She only has a frame of reference for how it used to look. Understand?"

"Hell, no," Flynn said.

Nate Pierce swept past where they were standing with the GPR. "Welcome to my world," he said, then held out his hand. "I want to shake the hand of the guy with the guts to take this female on. I'm Nate Pierce. Assistant professor of geology at the university, and the loser of a bet between me and the witch doctor, thus the reason I am here."

Flynn grinned and all the bluster drained out of him in the face of the older man's irritation. "Flynn O'Mara. Nice to meet you."

"See. It's no big deal." Tara kissed the side of Flynn's cheek.

"Not that I'm complaining, but what was that for?" Flynn asked.

"I never had anyone get jealous before. It's kind of a rush."

He grinned. "You are so crazy."

Before Tara could answer, Henry popped up in front of her and started waving his hands.

"Millicent?" she said, thinking of the earlier bubble disaster. Then she realized Nate had stopped. "OMG . . . did he—"

Henry pointed to his nose, as if he was playing charades and she'd guessed the clue, then disappeared.

"He found something." Tara started running.

Nate had squatted down closer to the radar and was staring at the computer screen.

"What? What? Did you find it?"

Nate shook his head. "The first hint of disturbance was visible on the previous two sweeps over this area, but I kept thinking it wouldn't pan out. But it showed up on the third sweep, too. The disturbance of soil is the right depth down for a grave. It's the right size. I can't believe this."

"Is it a grave?"

"I don't know what it is. But it's the right size and depth for a possible grave."

"Can you print that out for me?"

He nodded. "Oh yeah."

"Cool." Tara looked up to find DeeDee hovering nearby again. "Hang in there, honey," she said. "We're closing in."

"I'm sorry? What did you say?" Nate asked.

"I don't think she was talking to us," Flynn offered.

"Oh. Right." Nate stood abruptly and stared at Tara as if he was the one seeing ghosts. "You are something," he said. "I wish my Grandma Littlebird was still alive. She would be fascinated with you. In a good way, of course."

"Whatever." Tara pointed at the screen. "Is that it, DeeDee? Can you tell?"

The little ghost hovered over the area, then disappeared. Tara didn't know what that meant, and DeeDee obviously wasn't talking.

"Okay. I've got a phone call to make," she said.

"Who to," Flynn asked.

"The police, of course. They have to find a body before they can begin an investigation, and I promised DeeDee justice. She's never crossed over because of all this."

"Sorry I asked," Flynn mumbled.

Nate Pierce chuckled.

Tara glared at both of them. "Don't anybody leave. I might need a little backup from the professor before this is over."

Nate started to argue, then subsided. "Got any more of those cookies?"

Tara nodded as she pulled her cell phone out of her pocket, and pointed to Flynn. "Flynn, would you escort Nate into the kitchen? The cookies are on the cabinet in the cookie jar. Cold pop is in the fridge." She glanced at her watch. "Uncle Pat is due home any time. I am going to be explaining this a thousand times."

"Follow me," Flynn said to Nate.

Nate left with Flynn, leaving Tara alone to make her call.

Tara didn't know the number to the police station, so she had to go through information, which only made her more jittery when she finally connected.

"Stillwater Police Department," a man answered.

"I need to speak with Detective Rutherford of the Homicide Division, please."

"One minute," he said. A few seconds passed, then Tara heard Rutherford's voice.

"This is Rutherford."

"Detective Rutherford, this is Tara Luna, the girl who found Bethany Fanning. Remember?"

"I'm not likely to forget you," he said. "How can I help you? Oh wait. Let me guess. Since you've called Homicide, you must have found yourself a body, right?"

Tara gasped. "Oh wow!! How did you know? Are you psychic, too?"

There was a long, uneasy silence. For a few moments, Tara thought he'd hung up. "Detective! Hello? Are you there?"

"What the hell, excuse my language, do you mean?"

"There's a body buried in the backyard of the house where we live."

"And you know this because . . . "

"You don't want to know," she said. "But I have proof."

"Like what? A map?"

Tara frowned. "You are psychic, aren't you?"

"You have a map?"

"In a manner of speaking. Are you going to come out or not?"

"Right now? You expect me to believe all this crap, excuse my language, and show up at your house with a shovel or what?"

Tara resented the sarcasm and fired back with some of her own. "I expect you to investigate my claim, see the evidence, and hear what I have to say. We are tax-paying citizens of Stillwater, and I have just called you to report a crime. I expect you to respond to my cry for help. And if you're the one who does the digging in cases like this, then hell, yes, excuse *my* language, bring the shovel."

She didn't know Rutherford was grinning. All she heard was a sigh that sounded a little like submission.

He's going to come. He likes you. He just doesn't want you to know it.

Thank you, Millicent. That's something I needed to hear.

Finally, my information is being appreciated.

"Give me your address," Rutherford said.

Tara rattled off her address, then added. "If you don't mind, would you please hurry. I would like it if you were already here by the time Uncle Pat gets home from work. He doesn't know about the body in the back yard, and I may need some backup. It's been a long time since I got a spanking, but he might just reconsider after this bit of news."

"Hang tough, Xena. I'll be there shortly."

Tara grinned. Calling her Xena was kind of cool. She pocketed her cell just as Flynn and Nate came back outside. Within seconds, Uncle Pat came out behind them.

Run while you still have the chance.

Shut up, Millicent. I do not run away from Uncle Pat.

Don't say I didn't warn you.

Tara gulped. It wasn't often Millicent offered sympathy. Tara decided that a friendly offense was better than a whiny defense.

"Hi, Uncle Pat. Just in time."

"I'd like to ask, in time for what, but something tells me I'm not going to like the answer," he said.

Tara threw her arms around him and gave him a big hug. "Don't be mad. It's all good, and if everything works out like I think, then DeeDee, the ghost living in our house, will finally cross over."

Uncle Pat's eyebrows shot upward as his mouth slid open.

Tara decided now was the time for some formal introductions. "Uncle Pat, have you met Professor Pierce? He's from the university. This is his GPR we're using. Nate, this is my uncle, Pat Carmichael."

Nate shook Uncle Pat's hand. "Pleasure to meet you, sir," he said. "Even under these circumstances. Being responsible for a kid like Tara must be a challenge."

Pat managed a nod before focusing his attention back to Tara.

"I'll get you a drink, Tara." Flynn took one look at the expression on Pat's face and retreated back into the house.

"What, exactly, needs to take place here in our backyard so that this DeeDee can do her thing?" Pat asked.

"Here's the deal, Uncle Pat. DeeDee was murdered. She doesn't know for sure who killed her, but she knows she's buried out here somewhere."

Pat's mouth dropped. "In our backyard?"

Tara nodded. "Yep. Actually, her family once owned this house. She grew up here. I'm pretty sure her brother Emmit is the one who killed her because when I went to see him to ask about DeeDee, he claimed he didn't have a sister."

Nate gasped and stared at Tara as if she'd suddenly grown horns.

Pat blinked at her then sputtered, "You went to see a man you suspect murdered his sister by *yourself?*"

Flynn walked up with two cold drinks and handed one to Tara. Thinking he'd make a joke, he piped up with a "What did I miss?"

"Tara!" Pat yelled. "What in holy hell made you think it was okay to do that?"

Tara frowned. "Cursing does not become you."

His face turned a dark, angry red. "Do not get all prissy with me, here, Missy. Just because your legs got longer doesn't mean I'm no longer the boss in this family."

Tara handed the pop can back to Flynn, threw up her hands, then put her hands on her hips in a gesture of defiance as she took a step forward and yelled back.

"Well, if you hadn't been so unwilling to accept what I've been telling you about myself my *entire* life, I might have discussed the situation with you beforehand. But no. You wouldn't ever let me talk about what I saw, let alone help me understand it. So explain to me exactly why I should suddenly decide to bring you in on what is business as usual for me while you constantly reject that part of who I am?"

Tara saw the impact her words had on her uncle in his stark expression. She'd seen the exact same look on his face lots of times—just before he reached for a bottle of booze. Then he seemed to shake it off. She couldn't do the same now that the problem was on the table.

Uncle Pat started to hug her, but she threw up her hands and took an angry step back.

"Okay. You're right," Pat said. "I haven't exactly been willing to accept that you were just like Mom and Shirley."

"And you didn't even tell me they had the same gifts until you were forced to," Tara muttered.

"You mean there are more like her?" Nate asked.

Pat shook his head. "Not anymore. But all the women in my mother's family for as far back as anyone can remember were like Tara. They just . . . they just . . . knew stuff, okay? Shirley was my sister and Tara's mother. She died before Tara was one. I guess I thought if nothing was ever acknowledged, it might go away."

"Well, it didn't," Tara said firmly, then looked toward the back gate. "Oh, good. There's Detective Rutherford."

Pat gawked. "You called the police?"

Tara rolled her eyes. "How else is DeeDee going to get justice? Someone has to find her body, begin an investigation, and find her murderer before she can cross over. Dang . . . does anybody *ever* listen to me?" She stomped off toward the back gate to meet the detective.

When she flipped a glance back over her shoulder, Uncle Pat looked thoughtful, Nate looked about half impressed, and Flynn looked like he should have had hearts in his eyes like cartoon characters did when they fell in love.

Chapter Six

Only slightly mollified, Tara Luna scowled at Detective Rutherford instead of greeting him.

"Looks like the party started without me," Rutherford said.

Tara rolled her eyes. "Don't get me started." Then she switched emotions before he got the wrong idea. "Thanks for coming so quickly. The grave we found is over here."

"Wait!" Rutherford said.

"You can talk over there as easily as you can here, so if you're going to argue, you'll have to follow me."

Rutherford sighed, but appeared willing to let Tara call the shots, probably on the assumption that the quicker he heard her out, the quicker it would be over. Whatever. Once he saw what Nate had found, he'd understand.

As soon as Uncle Pat, Flynn, and Nate reached them Tara began introductions. "Guys, remember Detective Rutherford of the Stillwater Police? We met when Flynn, Davis and I found Bethany Fanning. Detective, you remember Uncle Pat and Flynn. But the man who keeps frowning at me is Professor Nate Pierce from OSU's geology department. He helped me find the location of the body."

Nate looked dumbfounded all over again. "Hey kid, are you talking about that high school girl who was kidnaped? You found her?"

"I am not a kid and yes, we did," she said.

"No, Tara. You found her," Flynn said. "And if we'd been five minutes later, her body would have been in Boomer Lake."

"No way," Nate said, eyeing Tara with newfound respect.

But Nate wasn't the only one surprised. Rutherford's ears pricked up when he realized there was a bonafide professor in on this.

Nate caught the detective's surprised expression and shrugged. "I lost a bet."

"Ah," Rutherford said, as if that explained it all.

Tara was tired of all the chit-chat. She waved her hand to get their attention. "Okay, here's the deal, and I want everyone to listen and please don't interrupt, 'cause I'm only going to say this one more time. Our house has a ghost. When she was alive, her family owned this house from 1946 through 1986, I think. Her name was Sarah Delores Broyles. She went by the name of DeeDee. She had an older brother named Emmit."

"How do you know all this?" Rutherford asked.

Tara frowned. "Obviously, you must be hard of hearing. I apologize. I'll say this once more. *No questions.* I know this from records at the court house," Tara added, then resumed her story. "As I was saying, according to the records, the brother and sister were joint heirs when their parents died. But soon after their deaths, DeeDee Broyles disappeared. No one reported her missing and suddenly Emmit was the sole owner. So I went to see Emmit and—"

The detective's mouth dropped, and he glared at Tara's uncle. "What the hell, excuse my language, were you thinking to let her do that?"

Tara frowned. "Don't yell at Uncle Pat. He didn't know until a few minutes ago and I'm still talking. *So* I went to see Emmit. His wife, Flora, came to the door. I told her I'm living in Emmit's old family home and had a question I wanted to ask. When I mentioned Emmit's sister, she told me he didn't have one. Well, I already knew that wasn't true. So then Emmit came to the door. I ask him the same question and he told me he didn't have one and to get out. For an old man, he's pretty scary. He's huge, and he's been stalking me ever since."

At this point, Uncle Pat went ballistic. His face turned red and he threw his hands up in disbelief. "Tara! For the love of—"

Tara kept on talking. "Emmit has a key to our house. He actually came inside and walked all through the rooms looking for me because he knew I was here. But I was hiding in Uncle

Pat's closet and just as he opened the door, DeeDee appeared and scared him away."

"Tara Luna! You are so grounded!" Pat yelled.

Tara didn't flinch. Being grounded wasn't bad. It just meant she stayed home, and she liked being home. She just had no intention of letting Uncle Pat know. He needed to think he still held some kind of authority over her.

Flynn was staring at Tara as if she was a stranger.

Rutherford was hearing her, but obviously finding it difficult to believe such a convoluted story. Still, he kept his mouth shut and let her talk.

Nate was starting to get it. Tara could tell from the calm in his voice.

"Then what happened?" he asked.

"Thank you for your interest," Tara said. "It scared me, but I think Emmit was scared more by seeing his sister's ghost. That's how I knew he wouldn't come back here. It has not stopped him from stalking me off the premises, though. Detective, if you check the records for accidents here in Stillwater, you'll find that Emmit Broyles recently had a run-in with a semi at the Hall of Fame intersection just east of Mexico Joe's. At that time, he'd been following me. Millicent spotted him and warned me he was behind me. Then she stopped his car in the intersection which caused the semi to hit it."

"Who's Millicent?" Rutherford said.

"You don't want to know," Uncle Pat muttered.

Tara kept talking. "So then a few days later, I was in the back yard and looked up and saw him driving down the alley over there."

Pat freaked again. "Where was I? Why don't I know any of this stuff?"

Tara shrugged. "You were at work, Uncle Pat. Besides, I always have Henry and Millicent."

Rutherford frowned, repeating his earlier question. "Who's Millicent? Who's Henry?"

"I told you, you don't want to know," Uncle Pat said.

"Sadly, I do," Rutherford said.

"They're ghosts. They've been with me for years," Tara said.

Rutherford's eyes bugged. "Son of a bitch, excuse my language, are they here? Now?" He turned in a nervous circle.

Tara tilted her head, as if listening, then she waved a hand. "I don't hear Millicent. I saw Henry earlier, but he's not around right now."

"Well, that's good to know," Rutherford muttered, then pointed at Tara. "What happened after you saw Emmit Broyles coming down the alley?"

Tara nodded. "Right. Well, I think he meant to be sneaky. You know, see what was going on without being spotted, but I was in the back yard. Henry warned me something was up, and then Millicent filled in the blanks. That's when I saw Emmit. When he saw me, he freaked out and started to accelerate, but he got flustered, hit the brakes instead, and had himself another mini-wreck. Smashed his face against the steering wheel, the whole thing. He probably had to get stitches. You could check the emergency room records."

"Most likely . . . and a good idea," Nate drawled.

"Don't encourage her," Pat said.

Nate shrugged. "Just helping the saga along. I want to hear the end of it, and I usually go to bed around 10:00 p.m."

It wasn't even dark, and Tara was tired of their snide remarks. "None of you are funny," Tara said. "This isn't easy for me, either, you know. Now. Where was I?"

"Emmit was getting stitches," Nate said.

"Right. So DeeDee is sad and angry and everything in between. She hasn't been able to cross over and she wants justice. I told her I'd find out where she was buried, and then the police could open an investigation and go from there. So Nate, I mean Professor Pierce, just found the grave. I could have just dug her up myself, but I didn't want to mess up what I know is going to become a crime scene. I watch CSI. I know the rules."

Rutherford looked at Nate, then pointed at the wheeled contraption beside him. "And this is where you and that thing come in?"

Nate nodded. "I told you before, I lost a bet. So I said I would bring the GPR and do a scan of her backyard. GPR stands for Ground Penetrating Radar. It's used for all kinds of reasons besides identifying possible pockets of oil or natural gas."

"Like identifying graves?" Rutherford asked.

Nate shrugged. "It doesn't necessarily show what's there, just that the earth has been disturbed, and the size and depth of the disturbance. I'll be honest, I didn't think anything would be here. I'm as surprised as the rest of you, but what we found certainly fits the possibility of it being a grave."

"So show me," Rutherford said.

Nate turned around, squatted beside the GPR, then pointed at the laptop screen and began to explain what they were seeing.

Tara watched the detective's expression go from irked to curious, then from curious to disbelief.

Suddenly, he turned and stared at Tara as if he was the one who'd just seen a ghost. "You do know I will verify everything you've told me before a blade of grass gets turned."

Tara nodded. "And you do know that when Emmit Broyles gets wind of what's going on, he's going to disappear."

Rutherford sighed. "I'll put a man on him just in case."

Tara wasn't satisfied. "The courthouse is still open. Have someone check the ownership records for this property. Have someone else check the census records for back then. As I said, Sarah Delores Broyles, who went by the name of DeeDee, is listed as a sister—the sister Emmit swears he never had."

Rutherford shoved a hand through his hair in frustration. "Damn it, girl, excuse my language, am I going to have to put you on the payroll to get you off my back?"

"No. Just find DeeDee, then find her killer," Tara said softly. She gave them all a sweeping glance. "I think I'm done here. I'm tired of arguing. I'm sad for DeeDee and I feel sorry for myself that I'm not some shallow-minded teenager who's biggest problem is not having enough money to buy herself a real Gucci purse instead of a knock-off."

"Well?" Nate asked. "She's right. It won't take long to check records. If that man denies ever having a sister and he did, that's damning. And if he never reported her missing, and she was, that's even worse. I'd be seriously suspicious . . . if I were you."

Rutherford glared. "What are you, her agent?"

Tara rolled her eyes again, but Nate answered before she could.

"No," Nate said, "but I can say with all honesty, this has been one of the most amazing days of my life, and I'm sticking around to see how it ends."

Pat nodded. "It goes without saying that I'm on Tara's side. She's special in so many ways, and you have to remember, I grew up with women like her. They were always right."

"Always?" Rutherford asked.

"Always."

Tara was grateful for Uncle Pat's conviction.

Rutherford nodded and pointed at Nate. "Get me a print-out of that." Then he pointed at Pat. "Find something and mark this area. I've got some phone calls to make, and I have to find a way to explain all this to the Captain before I can get Forensics out here."

"How long before you begin digging?" Tara asked.

Rutherford stared down at the ground, as if trying to see what lay beneath. "Between you and me, if I had a shovel, I'd start right now. But Tara's right. This has to be dealt with in a scientific manner. A lot of years have come and gone since the body—if it's here—was buried. We're looking at serious decomposition. Without having been buried in a casket, there's no way of telling of what we may or may not find."

"The bones will be there," Nate said.

Pat smiled. "Ah, a convert."

"She made a believer out of me yesterday," Nate said.

Tara smiled and snuck a look at Flynn, who was staring at her with hot eyes.

Rutherford shook his head and headed for his car. Nate

followed with the GPR. He needed to take it back to the University, then hook his laptop to a printer and get Rutherford what he needed.

Pat got a can of red spray paint and marked off the spot.

Tara looked around for DeeDee. "Everything's going to come out, now," she said to the air.

Flynn raised an eyebrow. "Is she here?"

"I don't see her. But maybe. This is what she's been waiting for."

Tara was sitting at the kitchen table with her head in her hands. Flynn stood on the other side of the room, uncharacteristically quiet. Millicent floated in a pink cloud on the other side of the table.

They meant well.

Tara heard her, but she was mentally exhausted. She didn't respond to Millicent, but when Flynn, who was hovering near the back door, shuffled his feet nervously, she looked up.

"Flynn, you're making me nervous. Sit down, okay?"

He crossed the floor and slid into a seat beside her, then slid his hand up the back of her neck and massaged it gently.

"It's been a rough day, hasn't it, Moon girl?"

She nodded. Then the room disappeared in a blur of tears.

Flynn groaned. "Don't cry," he begged.

"I'm not crying," Tara said. "My eyes just burn, that's all."

"Just so you know . . . I think you're amazing. I don't understand how you do it, but your heart is so in the right place."

"Thanks," Tara said, and then leaned her head on his shoulder and sighed. "It's been a long day. I didn't want to go to bed tonight without knowing the search for justice for DeeDee had begun."

"Well, you've already accomplished that," Flynn said.

Tara nodded, then to her surprise, started to cry. Slowly at first, and then more and more until she was out and out sobbing. She cried for herself and how hard it was just to be in her shoes, and for all the lost souls she kept seeing who didn't have the closure they needed to cross over. She worried about being able to stay strong enough to help them and still live her own life. She wondered if the stress of it all would finally wear her down until there was nothing more substantial left of her than there was of the ghosts she saw.

When Pat came in and found Tara crying, he pulled her out of the chair and into his arms.

"Don't cry, honey," he said softly. "Don't cry. We're gonna help you find your little DeeDee. I promise."

Tara was too tired to be embarrassed that she was bawling like a baby in front of Flynn.

"Thanks, Uncle Pat," she said, and then hugged him fiercely.

"Yeah, Tara. We're all gonna help you," Flynn said.

"Just promise me something," Pat added. "If Emmit Broyles comes near you again, tell me. Tell Flynn. Tell Rutherford. Tell everyone . . . do you hear me?"

"I promise," Tara said, and then wiped her eyes and blew her nose on the handkerchief Uncle Pat gave her.

At that point, there was a knock on the back door.

"I'll get it," Flynn said, opened the door to find Detective Rutherford at the front door.

"I need to talk to the kid," he said.

"We all made her cry. Do not amp up the disbelief again," Flynn said shortly.

Rutherford looked startled, then scrubbed a hand across his face. "I'm sorry. This has been an off day for me in more ways than one. However, I still need to talk to her."

Rutherford followed Flynn into the kitchen just as Tara was washing her face at the sink.

"Hey, kid. We got lucky."

"How so?" Tara asked.

"My Captain, Adam Farrell, had grandparents who used to live in that yellow house across the street. He was a little kid, but he distinctly remembers a man and woman living here. He thought they were married because their last names were the same, but he remembers his grandmother always talked about how nice DeeDee was, and how she always brought her the extra cookies when she baked. In fact, he remembers trick or treating at the house one Halloween when DeeDee passed out popcorn balls in the shape of little pumpkins."

"No way!" Tara cried.

"Way," Rutherford said, grinning. "So we have a Forensic team on the way as we speak." He glanced at Pat. "Hope you have good lighting out back. If not, we'll be stringing some search lights."

"You're going to start this evening?" Pat asked.

"Yeah. Captain was pretty adamant. He's already sent a car to pick up Emmit Broyles and bring him in for questioning."

"He believed me?"

"It was Emmit's wife who cinched it. When the officer we sent out asked her the whereabouts of her husband's sister, she said we were mistaken because he didn't have one. That sort of tipped the scales in your favor."

"Whatever it takes." Tara saw movement from the corner of her eye. It was DeeDee, and for the first time Tara had felt happiness in her. She smiled. DeeDee smiled back, then faded away.

"Soon," Tara promised.

"Yeah, you're right," Rutherford said, thinking Tara had been talking to him. "If that body is there, it won't take long to find out if it's DeeDee. There might be dental records or a DNA match to Emmit, or maybe—"

Tara's eyes narrowed as DeeDee slipped an image into her head. "You'll find a necklace with the body. A locket, with the initials SDB inside."

"You're kidding?"

"I do not kid about ghosts."

"Man, if you're right, your skills could come in real handy in homicide."

Tara held up her hands and took a step backward. "I also do not plan to go out looking for anymore murders any time soon, thank you very much."

"It was just a thought," Rutherford said. "However, I'm afraid we're going to be making a lot of racket for most of the night."

Pat slid a comment into the conversation. "I just realized you might want to talk to our landlord. His name is Gene Whiteside. He owns Whiteside Realty."

"I know Gene," Rutherford said. "I'll give him a call." Then he added. "I know it's an imposition, but will it be all right if I tell the guys they can use your facilities when necessary?"

"You talking about the bathroom?" Pat asked.

"Yeah, and maybe water from some outside faucets. That kind of thing."

"Whatever you need," Pat said, and then gave Tara a conspiratorial wink. "If you allow us access to watch if we want."

Rutherford nodded. "I think that can be arranged."

Tara sighed. Uncle Pat knew just what to ask. It wasn't that she wanted to see what was left of DeeDee's body, but she felt like she had to. Someone needed to grieve for her, even if it was a few decades late.

Tell them to bring Emmit here. He'll spill his soup.

Tara resisted the urge to grin. Millicent never got slang right. *You mean he'll spill his guts. But you're right.*

"Uh, Detective Rutherford, if you bring Emmit Broyles to this house, I think he'll confess, which would save you a lot of time and money running DNA tests and looking for dental records, right?"

Once again, Rutherford was stunned. "Why would coming here—"

"I think DeeDee will probably scare him into confessing."

"You're kidding, right?"

"Nope. Just dig her up and show him the remains. That oughta do it."

Rutherford grinned and shook his head as another knock sounded at the front door. "That's probably the Forensic crew," Rutherford said. "I'll get them started and we'll go from there."

"I'll go with you," Pat said, and followed the detective out.

Flynn looked at Tara, then put his arms around her and pulled her close.

"You are so amazing," he said softly.

"For a lunatic, I guess I'm not half bad," Tara said, and then laid her head on his shoulder and hugged him back. It felt good to have backup.

The number of police cars in front of the little house on Duck Street, the yellow crime scene tape that had been strung, and the Forensic van pulled up to the back gate caused an uproar in the neighborhood. By evening, a small crowd had gathered across the street, trading gossip about what might be happening, while the traffic in front of Tara's house had increased three-fold.

Flynn had gone to Eskimo Joe's to catch his Mom up on what was happening and come back with burgers and fries. Nate Pierce had come back. He spent half his time watching the police, and the other half watching Tara's reactions to what was going on. She was aware that her ability to communicate with spirits fascinated him. She sensed he believed her, but as a scientist who dealt in facts that could be counted and analyzed, what she knew seemed impossible.

Tara tried to concentrate on homework, but it was impossible. She'd made half a dozen trips from the house to the dig site, and each time she'd gone outside, she'd seen DeeDee hovering somewhere nearby. Poor DeeDee. How bizarre would it be to watch your own bones being dug up? Even worse—OMG—how awful would it be to know all that was left of you were bones? Ugh.

She'd spoken to Nate Pierce a couple of times and offered him food, although he politely refused. The growing pile of dirt was encouraging, but the time they were taking was maddening. She understood the need not to damage evidence, but it was making her crazy. She also knew the crowd across the street was becoming a traffic issue. Between the extra cars parked along the curbs and the people who'd come out of their houses, it was absolutely nuts. She could only imagine what they must be thinking.

Finally, she saw Flynn's car coming down the street, and ran across the yard and out the back gate to meet him. Before Flynn could park, Prissy and Mel, two of the girls who'd taken joy in making the first week of her life at Stillwater High a living hell, drove by in Mel's car, gawking like everything. When Tara caught them looking at her, they turned their heads and accelerated. She sighed. No telling what kind of gossip was going around now. After all, she *was* the lunatic of Stillwater High.

"Hope you're hungry," Flynn said, as he got out of the car. "The burgers and fries smell good enough to eat."

Tara nodded. "I could eat a little."

Flynn frowned when she didn't respond to his joke. "I'm sorry. Didn't mean to put down the seriousness of what's going on here."

Tara shook her head and then smiled. "It's okay. Let's just get inside. All these people staring makes everything so intense."

Flynn glanced over his shoulder at the people pointing and talking, even though no one seemed willing to be caught looking. He frowned. "Yeah. No wonder you're bummed. Come on, Moon girl. Let's go inside."

They went into the house, and Tara locked the door behind her. The police were coming and going through the back gate or coming into the house though the kitchen door. There was no need to leave easy access to anyone else.

"I'll get the food onto plates. You go get your uncle," Flynn said.

"Right." Tara hurried outside to where Pat was standing. She slid her hand under his elbow, then whispered, "Flynn's here with supper."

"Good," Pat said. "As gruesome as this is, I'm surprised that I'm actually hungry."

"I know. I think it's because she's been gone so long ago that it doesn't seem real," Tara said, then glanced at DeeDee, who was now hovering in the corner of the yard next to the old arbor. "Although, I guess for DeeDee, it might as well have been yesterday."

Pat took her by the hand and led her away. "You have such a tender heart. This will be a tough night. Man, that smells good," he said, as he walked into the kitchen. "Let me wash up and I'm there."

He went straight to the kitchen sink and grabbed the soap, while Tara began fixing glasses with soft drinks.

"Hey, Flynn, what's Mona think about all this?" Pat asked.

Flynn shook his head. "She said she's just glad this isn't our back yard."

Pat frowned. "I can only imagine. She's a little squeamish anyway. This would probably send her over the edge."

Tara didn't miss her uncle's familiarity. Obviously, he and Flynn's mom were getting even closer. She didn't know how that was going to play out, but could see it becoming messy. What on earth would she do if Uncle Pat and Mona got married? Could she and Flynn actually find themselves having to live together—like stepbrother and stepsister? Bad vibes all around on that scenario.

Flynn brought the food to the table. "I don't think they sent napkins."

"Get some paper towels," Tara said, pointing to the roll beside the sink. "And get the ketchup out of the fridge, will you?"

He nodded. "Sure. It's freaky sitting down to burgers and fries while the cops are in the back yard digging up a body."

"Tell me about it," Tara said.

She watched the men eating, talking and arguing about an upcoming football game at T. Boone Pickens stadium on campus. OSU was playing Missouri. She wasn't much of a football fan, but from the way Flynn was talking, he was. And her Uncle Pat liked to watch anything that involved team competition. She was so out of the loop here it wasn't funny.

But then she'd been out of the loop from the day she was born.

I get you.

Tara sighed. *Thank you, Millicent. I get you, too.*

Henry popped up in the middle of the table, sitting cross-legged beside the salt and pepper and blew Tara a kiss.

She laughed out loud. OMG—if the guys knew what was going on under their noses, they would freak.

Flynn looked up, smiled at her and winked, thinking she was laughing at something they'd said. Tara giggled even more, and took another bite of burger. The light moment gave her mood a much-needed boost.

They finished their meal, then Tara hit her homework. Flynn went home, Uncle Pat went back outside, and someone knocked on the door.

Tara started not to answer, then thought it might be a policeman and went to the door.

To her horror, she saw people getting out of a news van with a video camera and freaked. She slammed the door and locked it, then booked it through the house on the run. Once outside, she began yelling.

"Uncle Pat! Uncle Pat! There is a news crew on our front porch."

Pat frowned.

"I'll handle that," Detective Rutherford said, and winked at Tara. "Don't worry, kid. It comes with the territory when you're famous."

"I don't want to be famous," Tara said. "I just want justice for DeeDee." Then she stomped back into the house and slammed the door.

Whatever Detective Rutherford said to the news crew seemed to satisfy them. A few minutes later, they were gone. Then night came, and the crowd across the street went home, hoping the local news would cover what was going on at the house on Duck Street.

Tara fell asleep on the living room sofa, too worn out to stand any longer beside the deepening hole. But Uncle Pat stayed, and to Tara's surprise, he stayed sober.

It was twenty minutes after two in the morning when Uncle Pat woke Tara to tell her they'd found the first bone. One minute there'd been nothing but dirt beneath their feet, and then another careful shovelful of dirt was removed and someone yelled, "I've got something."

Tara moved to the edge of the hole, watching as the investigator went down on his knees and began moving dirt with his hands until what had once been DeeDee Broyles' forehead was revealed. The skull was small, and oddly pitiful to view. Tara realized what a tiny person she must have been.

Uncle Pat and Nate Pierce stood beside her staring down into the hole. All of a sudden, Nate looked up like he heard something in the air above him. Then he caught Tara's eye.

"You were right," he said.

"I know," she said, her voice breaking.

Chapter Seven

Sometimes it sucked to be right. Tara stood beside the open grave, her arms wrapped around herself even though it was a warm night. She wished she could wrap her arms around DeeDee.

Suddenly, Tara looked up and caught Detective Rutherford staring at her. He stood with his hands in his pockets, shaking his head in disbelief.

"It's time," she said.

"For what?" Rutherford asked.

"Get Emmit."

He glanced down at the skeleton slowly being revealed, then nodded. "Yeah."

He took a cell phone out of his pocket and made a quick call. Since the police were still holding Emmit Broyles at the precinct for questioning, it was simple to get him here.

"Has Emmit said anything?" Tara asked, when Rutherford hung up.

"Denied the whole thing. Claims the only reason he says he doesn't have a sister is because she ran away with a bunch of hippies when she was young. Says he hasn't heard from her in years and doesn't know where she is."

"But we do, don't we?" Tara said softly.

"Sure looks like it," Rutherford said, then glanced at his watch. "They'll be here soon."

Tara looked back into the hole, staring at the skull, arm bones, and the partially revealed ribcage of DeeDee Broyles. "She's not going anywhere." Then DeeDee popped up beside Tara, swamping her with emotional gratitude. "At least not for a while," she added.

Nate joined them, and they all stood guard above the hole,

waiting for DeeDee's resurrection and Emmit's arrival.

Fifteen minutes later, two uniformed officers came through the back gate with Emmit Broyles between them. Emmit was already uneasy, but when he saw the lights strung up across the back yard, and that they were excavating, he stopped.

"Bring him over!" Rutherford called, but Emmit wasn't moving.

The two officers grabbed Emmit's arms and forcibly pulled him forward.

Uncle Pat put a hand on Tara's shoulder. "Good Lord, Tara. You weren't kidding when you said he's scary. He's huge. I can't believe you faced him down alone."

Nate just shook his head. "You're going to be something else again when you're all grown up."

Tara was entirely focused on Emmit. She could feel his panic and the sickness in his belly, but she had no sympathy for any of it. All of her sympathies were with DeeDee.

"You have no right to treat me this way," Emmit roared, and struggled to get free.

"There's something we want you to see." Rutherford pointed down into the pit.

It appeared as if Emmit would faint. He staggered, then pulled himself together and walked forward. When the officers reached the edge of the grave, they stopped.

Emmit wouldn't look down. Instead, he glared across at Tara.

Now she felt something besides fear. His rage at what she'd done was huge. If he could have gotten to her, he would have put his hands around her neck and squeezed.

All of a sudden, Tara gasped. That was it! That's how he had killed DeeDee. He grabbed her from behind and broke her neck. But why? The house was small. Even when it was new, it wasn't like it would have been worth any kind of fortune. What could he have hoped to gain from her death?

He was stealing money from his job and DeeDee found out.

Tara gasped. Oh my God. Millicent was amazing. Tara met Emmit's gaze without flinching, waiting for him to come undone.

Rutherford pointed down into the pit. "We found a skeleton in what used to be your backyard," he said.

Emmit wouldn't look.

"Lots of people have lived here since I did," he said abruptly.

"We have reason to believe the body belongs to your sister, DeeDee," Rutherford said.

"My sister ran away from home years ago," he said, refusing to budge from his earlier story.

"That's not what we think happened here," Rutherford said. "We think you killed your sister in a fit of rage and hid her body in the backyard of the property that belonged to the both of you."

"That's a lie!" Emmit still wouldn't look down.

Tara felt Uncle Pat move closer to her. Through all this mess, he'd surprised her by how amazing he'd been. He hadn't once turned to alcohol and even though he had grounded her, he was still fiercely protective.

Rutherford continued to push. "Mr. Broyles, my question to you is, why would you kill your sister?"

Emmit turned on them all with a roar, screaming every word that came out of his mouth. "How many times do I have to tell you, I did not kill my sister!"

"You're finally admitting you have one?" Tara said. "Then why did you lie to me when I asked you about her?"

Rutherford frowned. "Tara, I'm the one doing the—"

"You're nothing," Emmit shouted. "Why would I talk to you? Why would you need to know anything about my personal life?"

She hadn't. DeeDee had sought justice. Tara spoke on her behalf because no one else could.

She yelled back at Emmit, as loudly as he'd yelled at her. "I told you that when I went to your house, remember? I told you the house was being haunted. You freaked because you knew who would be haunting it, didn't you? Then you came to our house. You unlocked the front door and walked into a house that no longer belonged to you. You were trespassing. And you were looking for me. Why? Were you going to kill me, too? But you didn't get the chance, did you? You opened that closet door and got more than you bargained for, didn't you, Emmit?"

The derision in her voice dug at Emmit Broyles like an itch he couldn't scratch. "Shut up! Shut up! I don't know what you're talking about!"

Tell them to look at the keys on his key ring.

Tara's eyes widened. Again, Millicent to the rescue. She pointed at Emmit. "Detective Rutherford, if you would check the key ring in his pocket, I think you'll find a key on it that will open our front door."

Emmit jumped backward, but both officers grabbed him.

Rutherford held out his hand. "Mr. Broyles, kindly hand over your keys, please."

"You can't make me!" Emmit shouted. "Now, either arrest me or let me go."

"Fine with me," Rutherford said. "Arrest him."

Emmit blanched. "No. Wait. I wasn't—"

"Your keys. Hand me your keys," Rutherford said.

Emmit threw them at the detective, who handed them to an officer. "Go see if any of these will open the front door."

The officer nodded, and quickly left.

They didn't have long to wait. Within a minute or so, he came outside and waved at them from the porch.

"Yes. He has a key that unlocks the front door," the cop said.

Rutherford turned back to Emmit. "How do you explain that?"

But before Emmit could come up with a lie, he suddenly threw up his hands and screamed.

Tara flinched. DeeDee had appeared out of nowhere and was now hovering over the hole above her remains. Oh, wow! This was just what she'd been waiting for.

"Keep her away from me!" Emmit screamed, and tried to run. Again, the officers grabbed him, this time cuffing his hands together as they finally subdued him.

"Miss Luna is nowhere near you," Rutherford said, thinking Emmit was talking about Tara.

But DeeDee continued to float closer.

Emmit screamed again, and then dropped to his knees. "Stop. Stop. Stay away from me!"

Rutherford frowned in confusion. He glanced at Tara, who was calmly watching from the other side of the pit. "Tara, what the hell, excuse my language, is going on here?"

"DeeDee. She's here, and making sure Emmit can see her."

"Oh, man," Nate said. "And I thought this couldn't get any wilder."

Rutherford's eyes widened and his mouth dropped. He spun abruptly, looking wild-eyed around the area. "I don't see anything."

"Broyles does," Nate said.

The man was face down on the ground with his cuffed hands above his head, bawling like a baby. "Make her go away. Make her go away," he kept begging.

Tara escaped Uncle Pat's hold and circled the pit. She walked up behind Emmit, coming to a stop at his feet. "You have to tell the truth. She's waited all these years for justice, and she's not leaving until you tell the truth."

Emmit screamed, pounding the ground with his cuffed fists. "She was my sister and she was going to tell. It wasn't right! It wasn't right! I begged her! But she said no. It wasn't my fault. She should have kept quiet."

Nate gasped again. "Emmit Broyles really did kill his sister."

Rutherford grunted as if he'd just been kicked in the stomach. "You killed her because she was going to tell on you?" he barked. "What on earth did she have on you that was worth killing for?"

"He was stealing from his employer," Tara said. "She found out."

"Yes! Yes!" Emmit said. Then he groaned and rolled up in a ball on his side. "I did it. I'm sorry, I'm sorry."

"Trouble is, he's not sorry he killed his sister," Tara said softly. "He's just sorry he got caught."

"Yeah, that's my read on the situation, too," Rutherford said, and pointed at the man on the ground as he spoke to his officers. "Get him up. Emmit Broyles, you have the right to remain silent. You have the right to an attorney. If you cannot afford one, one will be—"

The detective's words faded into the background as Tara focused on DeeDee's frail spirit. She was still floating above Emmit's body, but she was fading. Tara wanted to cry, but she told herself this wasn't a bad thing. It was good. DeeDee was finally free to cross over. All she had to do was leave. But it felt to Tara as if she didn't know how.

"Turn around," Tara said softly. "All you have to do is turn around and then follow the light."

DeeDee held out her hands to Tara. It looked as if she was begging, but Tara knew differently. She was saying thank you the only way that she could.

Tara felt her joy as vividly as she'd once felt her sadness. "OMG, DeeDee, you have to stop or you're gonna make me cry."

The little ghost turned into a swirl of mist, and then she was gone.

Tara's vision blurred, but she swiped away her tears, watching Emmit Broyles being led away. Then she turned back to the pit and drew a shuddering breath at the sight below. They'd dug away enough dirt so that DeeDee's complete skeleton was revealed. She felt cold all the way to her soul. Such a waste of a precious life.

When the Forensic team found the locket Tara had mentioned, with the initials SDB on the inside, all doubts anyone had vanished.

Nate Pierce picked up his jacket, nodded once to Tara, then walked away.

Uncle Pat suddenly appeared at Tara's elbow. She leaned against his shoulder, taking comfort in the warmth of someone living as she stared blindly at the tiny white bones. So sad. So sad. But Sarah Delores Broyles had justice at last.

"We see you, DeeDee. We see you. You're not missing anymore."

Tara didn't bother to go back to sleep after Emmit's arrest. The Forensic team and the coroner were in the back yard until just after seven a.m. There was crime scene tape on the property, and the hole that they'd dug was still open when she went into the kitchen to make coffee.

Their landlord, Gene Whiteside, had been horrified by the revelation, but he had no idea of Tara's involvement in the discovery. Rutherford was keeping the media in the dark about it, too. The story was going to be that, during an ordinary plumbing crisis, the digging in the back yard had revealed bones. At that point, the people on the property had notified the police, who'd taken over from there.

The vagueness of the details might have brought further questions, except for the hubbub about Emmit Broyles' arrest. He'd long been a citizen in high standing, once a member of the City Council, and a long-time member of the Elks Lodge and the local country club. His wife, Flora, had fainted upon hearing the news and had been taken to Stillwater Medical Center.

For Tara, it was back to business as usual. Even though Uncle Pat had given her permission to stay home from school if she wanted, she'd opted to resume her normal routine. She'd put on an old pair of jeans, a short midriff length black tee, and her favorite pink hoodie. She pulled her hair back just like Angelina Jolie, and called herself good to go. Then she packed her books in her backpack and headed off to school.

Dozens of kids that she knew passed her in their cars on the way to school but no one waved or offered her a ride. She wondered what it would be like to wake up knowing your every need, both physical and monetary, would be met every day, then made herself focus on reality. There were worse things in the world than not having a car, like dying and getting buried in your own backyard.

She caught more than one person watching her from their front porch as she walked by. She knew they were curious, but she just put her head down and kept on walking. They'd find out soon enough about what had happened from the TV and the newspapers.

She reached Husband Street where the high school was located and was surprised to find Flynn waiting for her at the corner. He was, as usual, beyond hot in a black and white tee and stone-washed Levis. His thick, dark hair brushed the neck of his shirt, and the skull and barbed wire tattoo showing below the sleeve gave him just enough flare of danger to be interesting, although she knew now it was just a facade. Flynn O'Mara was as honest and straight as they came.

When she saw him smile, her heart gave a bounce. She hadn't realized how fragile she was feeling until she felt his arms slide around her shoulder. He gave her a quick hug and kiss, then moved into step beside her.

"I heard you finally found her," Flynn said.

"Yes. Did Uncle Pat call your Mom?"

"With all the gory details, including how old man Broyles lost his cool."

Tara grinned. "That's one way of putting it."

Flynn sighed. "I would have liked to have seen that. The sorry ass. I can't believe he was stalking you, and you never said a word to me about it."

Tara shrugged. "So, what could you do? What could anyone do? Just telling the police he was stalking me wouldn't have proved anything. It would have been his word against mine, and you know how adults treat teenagers. We had to find DeeDee to prove there was a reason he wanted to shut me up."

"Still, I hate to think of you going through all that on your own."

Tara glanced up at him, and then grinned. "Just so you know . . . I'm pretty tough."

Flynn chuckled. "Was that a warning or just an

observation?"

"Whatever it needs to be," Tara said.

They walked a short distance without speaking, which Tara thought was so cool. How great was it that she could be with a guy and be so comfortable that she didn't have to talk if she didn't want to? Tara was getting high on love and feeling pretty good about the world when all of a sudden, she felt that dark, ugly feeling again. The one with a hate that spelled death. She glanced up, then all around, but saw nothing obvious. There was just the usual traffic on the streets and the usual kids walking to school like they were. She wished she could get a handle on it, but until she figured out who was doing it and what it meant, she was helpless. At least it was far enough away that it wasn't making her physically sick.

Flynn noticed Tara was preoccupied in some way, and frowning. "Everything okay?"

Tara shifted focus, letting go of the unwanted emotion, and nodded. "Absolutely,' she said, and then looked up.

Stillwater High was just ahead. Blue and gold streamers were hanging around the front doorway, and all the cheerleaders were decked out in full uniforms, bouncing around among the students who were gathering.

"What's up?" Tara asked.

"Homecoming. I guess they're firing up the school spirit. There'll be a pep rally tomorrow night. Can you come?"

"Oh. Probably. Maybe. Uncle Pat grounded me yesterday, remember? He may retract and he might not. But homecoming might be what saves me. Maybe everyone will be so keyed up about the game that they'll ignore the cop cars that were at our place all day and night."

Flynn frowned. "You think you're gonna get some flack about that?"

Tara arched an eyebrow. "Practically every kid in school drove past my house yesterday, and that's not usual, so I *know* there will be some. But hopefully, not much."

Brace yourself.

OMG. Millicent. *Are you serious?*

Don't worry. I've got your booty.

Tara suppressed a grin. *No. You're supposed to say, I've got your back.*

I thought your booty was back there, too.

Ha. *It is, but that's not . . . you don't . . . Oh, never mind. Whatever.*

Tara heard Millicent pop off in a huff.

Unaware that Tara had just had a conversation with a ghost, Flynn grabbed her hand, as if warning anyone who needed to know, that she was not alone. They walked up the steps and into the school.

Tara, Luna and Flynn walked into school holding hands. Bad luck put Prissy, who was still put out about getting kicked off the cheerleading team for cheating on a test, and feeling like all kinds of an outsider for not getting to wear the cheerleader outfit and be a part of the upcoming pep rally, squarely in their path. Prissy sent her embarrassment and anger spinning toward Tara.

"We saw the cops at your house," she said, as Tara and Flynn walked by. "Heard you all got busted for making Meth."

Of course a good dozen or so students heard the accusation, stared at Tara and Flynn, and then scuttled down the hall, anxious to spread the latest news.

Tara's mouth dropped. A short time ago, Prissy had been all buddy-buddy because she and Flynn had found Bethany, but now she was back to her miserable self again.

"You are so pathetic, Prissy," Flynn said. "Every time you open your mouth, stupid comes out."

Tara just rolled her eyes and kept on walking. She wasn't going to stand in the hall and justify herself to someone who was trying to take her misery out on everyone else. Besides, they'd all know the truth soon enough.

"Are you okay?" Flynn asked.

Tara grinned. Of course I'm okay. Imagine how stupid

she's going to feel when the truth gets out."

"Yeah, right," Flynn said.

"Okay . . . so I'll see you later," Tara said, as they reached her locker.

"Stay tough, Moon girl," Flynn said, then glanced up and down the hall, making sure no teachers were watching before giving her a quick goodbye kiss.

Tara's cheeks were still warm when she walked into first hour.

Mrs. Farmer, the first hour teacher, was writing assignment notes on the blackboard when she saw Tara come in. She looked a little startled, then smiled nervously before looking away.

Tara sighed. *Crap. Please tell me she doesn't believe all this gossip, too?*

She heard you got caught shoplifting and your uncle had to bail you out of jail.

"No way!" Tara said, then jumped, realizing she'd said that out loud.

A couple of students looked at Tara, then at each other before bursting into laughter. Tara rolled her eyes. Great. The day was promising to be a total disaster.

I'll handle this.

No, Millicent, no. *OMG, do not make a scene.*

But Millicent didn't respond, and Tara took her seat with trepidation, afraid of what was going to happen next.

Students continued to come in, and the closer it got to the last bell, the faster they were moving. One boy walked past her desk and whispered "crack head" under his breath as he passed. A couple of girls who sat a few desks behind her snickered as they walked past her, too. Even though she knew she had nothing to be ashamed of, she was surprised by how much all this hurt.

She opened her book and stared at the pages without knowing what was on them while her eyes burned with unshed tears. Finally, the last bell rang and the class began.

By noon, Tara was a bundle of raw nerves.

Flynn took one look at her when they met at her locker before lunch and said, "You're not okay, and don't pretend you are. I heard all the gossip, some of which even involved me robbing a quick mart and hiding out at your house before getting caught. I was almost flattered, but really, how stupid is that? If I'd robbed a store, then how come I'm out and walking around like anyone else? Gossip sucks."

Tara bared her teeth in a fake smile. "You can say that again."

"Okay—"

She put her hand over his mouth to stop him, and she couldn't help a little grin.

"I got a smile out of you," Flynn said. "It was worth it. Hey, I have to stop by the gym to get a new lock. I'll meet you in the cafeteria as soon as I'm done."

"I'll wait for you outside," she said.

Flynn was slow in showing up, so Tara went in on her own. She chose her food without care, wondering how she was going to manage to swallow the hamburger and fries she had on her tray. She was about to pass up dessert when someone slipped into the line behind her and poked her in the back.

"Hey, lunatic . . . pick the cake. If you don't want it, I do."

Tara's heart skipped a beat as she pushed her milk aside and slid the cake onto her tray. It was Nikki! *And she's talking to me.*

Nikki grinned. "I've been looking all over for you. Where have you been?"

"I've just been doing my thing," Tara said. "How about you?"

"Had a dental appointment this morning. Missed the first half of the day, so I'm just now getting to school. Oooh, this actually looks good," she said, as she pointed to the chicken nuggets and fries. "I'll have that." She added some a small bowl of jello and a brownie, and grabbed a carton of milk.

They got to a table, then sat. A couple of minutes later, Mac and Penny showed up with their trays and joined them.

Tara was waiting for the other shoe to fall. Surely they'd all heard the gossip. Surely they would ask. But when they didn't, she couldn't stand the suspense any longer.

"Well, aren't you going to ask me what was going on at my house yesterday evening and all through the night?"

Nikki swiped a french fry through the last of her ketchup, then pointed to Tara's tray.

"You gonna use that ketchup?"

"No, help yourself," Tara said.

"I don't need to ask," Nikki said, as she squeezed ketchup on the last of her fries. "I figure if you want to talk, you will. If you don't, it doesn't change my day." Then she grinned, making her almond-shaped eyes sparkle.

Mac licked salt off her fingers, then looked at Tara. "Gossip is stupid," she said. "As soon as I found out you and your Uncle weren't hurt in any way, I didn't think too much more about it."

Penny was more honest. "Well, I want to know, but I want to hear it from your lips."

Tara grinned. "Ha! Honesty. I didn't think it was possible."

The girls looked at each other, then burst out laughing.

Tara wiped her hands on her napkin, then shoved her tray aside and leaned forward.

"Okay. Here's the scoop, and you guys are getting it before it hits the papers and TV. We had a plumbing problem. Uncle Pat started digging in the back yard where the landlord said the lines would be, and guess what he found?"

"What?" they all asked.

"Bones. Human bones."

"NO WAY!" The shriek came from all three at the same time, causing everyone around them in the cafeteria to look.

"Way," Tara said. "So we called the police. They come out with the Forensic team."

"OMG, just like CSI?" Mac asked.

"Just like," Tara said. "And it gets better. They found an entire skeleton . . . of a young woman. There was a locket with the bones. It had the initials SDB on it. So they got to checking old records, and found out some people named Broyles used to own the property way back. So, long story short, this young woman named DeeDee Broyles never got reported missing, so no one knew she'd been murdered."

Nikki shuddered. "That's just awful. Do they know who did it?"

"Oh yeah," Tara said. "Her brother did it. She found out he'd been stealing money from his job and was going to tell so he killed her. Broke her neck."

Mac's mouth was hanging open, her eyes wide with disbelief. "I can't imagine how freaky that was, having a body buried in your backyard and all. Didn't you get scared?"

"Why?" Tara asked. "Ghosts can't hurt you. Only real people can hurt you."

Penny shuddered. "Still, it gives me the creeps."

"Yeah, most people feel that way," Tara said, without elaborating. She wasn't about to tell them that her two best friends, except for Uncle Pat, were ghosts.

"So, do we know where the brother is?" Nikki asked. "Is he even still alive? He must be pretty old."

"He's not only alive, he lives here in Stillwater. They arrested him last night after he admitted it."

"OMG," the girls said in unison. "That is so crazy. Are you serious?"

"Oh yeah," Tara said.

"So, what's his name?" Mac asked.

"Emmit Broyles."

Nikki squealed. "No way! I know him. He belongs to the same country club that my dad belongs to."

"Well, there aren't any country clubs where he's going," Tara said.

At that point, Flynn came toward them carrying his tray. "Got room for one more?"

"Sit, sit," Nikki said. "So, were you in on all that, too?"

Flynn looked at Tara and grinned. "You told them?"

"Of course, she told us," Nikki said. "BFFs tell each other everything."

Tara felt her heart skip a beat. She'd never been anyone's

BFF before.

Flynn nodded, as he took a bite of his sandwich. "I only got in on a part of it. I knew the body was there before I left, but I wasn't in on any of the digging, or the killer being arrested."

"So, basically, you missed everything, didn't you?" Nikki said.

Flynn grinned. "Basically."

Everyone laughed again, which made the students around them stare once more. Let them wonder, Tara thought.

A few minutes later, Tara and her friends carried their trays to the cleanup area, then headed out into the halls.

"I've got to finish a bit of homework," Nikki said. "See you when I see you."

Mac and Penny followed, because that's what they did best, leaving Tara and Flynn alone.

"Wanna go outside?" Flynn asked.

Tara nodded.

They started up the hall, and were almost out the door when the principal, Mrs. Crabtree came out of her office.

"Miss Luna, would you step into my office for a few minutes? I would like to talk to you."

Oh, great! Not her, too, Tara thought. She looked at Flynn, who shrugged then walked away, leaving Tara to follow the principal back into her office. Tara knew what she was going to ask, and she was ticked off that she felt it was even her business to ask.

"How are you this afternoon?" Mrs. Crabtree looked all around the room, as if expecting something to fly through the air.

"Fine."

Mrs. Crabtree frowned. "I don't like your tone, young lady."

Tara sighed. "Am I in trouble?"

"No, but—"

"Am I in here because you want to discuss my personal business?"

Mrs. Crabtree's face flushed a bright, angry red. "We've been hearing some—"

"*We* being the gossip mill in this school, or *we* being an adult who's already talked to the police?"

"Well. Now. Of course I didn't call the—"

"So, *we* is the gossip mill," Tara said.

Don't tell me to stop, because I'm not going to listen.

Tara sighed. Now they were both in for it. Obviously, Millicent didn't like the principal's attitude, and truthfully, neither did she.

A stack of files levitated into the air, then turned upside down, sending papers flying in every direction.

Mrs. Crabtree squealed like a pig with its tail caught in the barn door, then clapped her hands over her mouth.

Tara ignored what was happening, and started talking.

"No one at my house got arrested. Not me. Not Uncle Pat. Not Flynn. No one committed a crime there . . . at least not in the last twenty-five years, and no one who lives there is in trouble. We did not get arrested for making Meth, and Flynn did not rob a quick stop."

The pens on Mrs. Crabtree's desk shot straight up into the ceiling and stuck like darts in the soft fiber panels.

"Oh, dear lord," Mrs. Crabtree gasped, and staggered back against the wall.

"We had a plumbing problem," Tara said, as if nothing was happening. "Uncle Pat started digging to find the clog and found bones. Human bones."

"Help," Mrs. Crabtree said.

The top popped off a black Sharpie. Tara flinched. Oooh. Millicent was going for broke.

"We called the police." Tara winced as the pen flew toward Mrs. Crabtree. Before she could say stop, Millicent had drawn a perfect mustache on Mrs. Crabtree's upper lip.

OMG. OMG. It was all Tara could do not to laugh. So she took a deep breath and wound up the story.

"They found the skeleton of a woman who'd been murdered a long time ago. They arrested a man named Emmit

Broyles for murdering his sister. I don't know the rest of the details. You'll have to watch the evening news. Is there anything else you want to know?"

Mrs. Crabtree just shook her head and waved toward the door without speaking.

Tara turned around and walked out, letting the door slam behind her to let Mrs. Crabtree know she was still ticked. *Millicent, if I could high five you, I would so do it.*

I feel your pain.

Tara threw back her head and laughed. She was still laughing when she walked outside to look for Flynn.

Chapter Eight

Flynn had been watching for Tara to come out. When he saw her appear in the doorway, he came up the steps to meet her.

"You okay?" he asked.

Tara grinned. "I'm fine."

"What's so funny?" he asked.

"She ticked Millicent off," Tara said.

Flynn's eyes widened. "No way."

"Way," Tara said. "She tossed that office like a hurricane, and drew a mustache on Crabtree's upper lip with a Sharpie. It was all I could do not to laugh."

Flynn shuddered. "Remind me never to talk back to you."

Tara laughed out loud. "Yeah. Right. But don't worry. Millicent thinks you're hot."

Flynn's face flushed, but he was grinning. "Seriously?"

Tara nodded.

"That's intense," Flynn said.

"Naw. Just Millicent. So, let's find some shade."

"Absolutely," Flynn said.

Tara's heart was light. Her steps were sure and easy. The weight of knowing DeeDee's earthbound spirit was finally gone felt good. When Flynn slipped his hand in hers and gave it a quick squeeze, she felt like giggling. What a wild and crazy day.

They found a spot beneath one of the old trees and sat down on the grass and started talking.

"Hey Flynn, did you ever talk to your Mom about your Dad's cancer?"

"Oh. Yeah. I can't believe I didn't tell you. She freaked. Seriously. Then she called him. They talked for as long as he could talk, but when she was done, she seemed better."

"Do you know if they tied up those loose ends we talked about?"

"Yeah, actually, they did. Mom said later she was glad I'd told her, so you were right. Thanks."

Tara nodded. "Sure. I'm still sorry about the cancer, though. Is it inoperable?"

Flynn nodded, then looked away.

Tara sighed. "I'm so sorry, Flynn."

He nodded, but wouldn't look up. She knew he had tears in his eyes and was sorry she'd brought it up. But before she could change the subject, that feeling of hate hit her so hard she actually winced, as if she'd been physically hit.

Get inside.

Tara shuddered. "Uh . . . Flynn . . . we need to go in. Help me up."

Flynn looked startled. Tara knew her face was as white as a sheet. "Moon girl . . . are you sick?"

"Like at the bowling alley. Get me up."

Flynn was on his feet and pulling her up before she'd unfolded her legs. "Hang onto me," he said, and slid his arm around her waist and started toward the school. "Are you sick? Do you need your necklace?"

"Yes, I'm sick, and yes, I need it, but it's in my purse, and that's in my locker."

"Oh man, oh man, oh man," Flynn said, dragging her as fast as her legs would move.

"This has got to stop!"

Tara moaned as another wave washed over her, leaving her nauseous and shaky.

"Yeah, well, if you figure out how to do that, let me know."

"I'm sorry, Moon girl. I just meant . . . "

"I know," Tara said, as they reached the steps of the school. "It's just my lunatic life."

"Man," Flynn said, as they got inside the school. "Are you better?"

"Some. Mostly because we're farther away. Just let me lean against the wall for a minute, okay? I'm already the gossip girl today. If they see you dragging me down the hall, they'll be saying I got drunk during the noon hour."

"This is too crazy," Flynn said, and shoved his hands through his hair.

Tara frowned. "All you have to do is walk off," she said shortly.

Flynn frowned back. "I didn't say I wasn't going to help you. I just said . . . this is a crazy way to live."

And just like that, her feelings were hurt. It wasn't like being her boyfriend was the easiest trick in the book, but she'd thought he was tougher than this. "It's not like I have any choice in the matter, though, is it? Excuse me," Tara said, and pushed herself away from the wall and walked away.

Flynn frowned, then doubled up his fists and hit the sides of his legs as he walked in the other direction.

Tara's heart hurt. Her head hurt. Her feelings hurt. The only positive was that the feeling of hatred had disappeared. Still, if someone talked to her now she would burst into tears. And, as luck would have it, the first person she made eye contact with as she neared the lockers was Prissy.

Prissy smirked.

Tara glanced around. *Millicent?*

I see her.

Tara scowled. *If she opens her mouth—*

Thank you for the opportunity.

Tara kept on walking.

Prissy wasn't smart enough to keep her mouth shut. "Hey lunatic, how much does it cost to get bonded out of jail?"

Tara's eyes narrowed angrily. "You stole five dollars out of your mother's purse this morning."

All the color faded from Prissy's face. "How do you do that?"

"The better question would be . . . why did you do that?" Tara countered, and kept on walking. When she heard Prissy suddenly scream, she didn't look back. She didn't have to. She already knew what Millicent was doing.

All the lockers behind Prissy suddenly popped open and

everything inside them fell out. One of the teachers who was on hall duty came running, grabbed Prissy by the arm, and hauled her off to the office, thinking she'd popped the locks and dumped the contents.

Tara could hear Prissy trying to explain all the way up the hall. After what had happened to Mrs. Crabtree, she would probably believe Prissy, but it didn't matter to Tara. At least someone else was the topic of conversation besides her.

She went to her next class and slid into her seat without looking at anyone. She was so ticked. How had everything gone from happy to bad this fast?

Suddenly, Henry popped up, sitting cross-legged on her desk. He leaned over and gave her a ghostly hug.

Tara sighed. *Thank you, Henry. I love, you, too.*

He disappeared as quickly as he'd appeared, but Tara already felt better. Even if it was a little bit foggy—like Henry—foggy love was better than no love at all.

She made it through the class without crying, and then came face to face with Flynn in her last hour again. He kept trying to get her attention, but she wouldn't look at him. When the bell rang to dismiss school, Tara filed out ahead of Flynn and didn't look back. As she was walking through the parking lot, Nikki picked her up and gave her a ride home.

"Where's Flynn?" Nikki asked, as Tara got into the car.

"Probably hiding, just to make sure he doesn't have to face me again," Tara muttered.

Nikki frowned. "No way. Did you two have a fight?"

Tara shrugged. "It wasn't a fight. He just can't handle me and my life, that's all."

Nikki reached into her purse and pulled out a Hershey bar. "Here. Break into the chocolate. It fixes all kinds of pain."

Tara grinned as she peeled back the paper and broke off a couple of squares, then handed it to Nikki, who did the same.

"Mmm, good," Tara said.

"One thing's for sure," Nikki said. "Friends and lovers may come and go, but chocolate goes on forever."

Tara burst into laughter, and by the time Nikki pulled into

their driveway, Tara felt better again. Nikki was right. The world did not have to begin and end with Flynn O'Mara.

"Thanks for the ride," she said.

"See you tomorrow," Nikki said, then handed Tara the last bites of the Hershey. "Here, take this. You need it more than I do."

"I won't say no," Tara said, and popped the chocolate into her mouth as she got out. She stood in the driveway and waved until Nikki drove away, then went inside.

The yellow crime scene tape was still strung across the back yard. The hole had yet to be filled, but DeeDee had finally gotten some justice, and Tara's stalker was in jail. The world didn't have to be perfect. Right now, she'd take the status quo.

She turned on the television for company, then threw her backpack on the table, pulled out homework, and went to the fridge. She couldn't do homework without a Dr. Pepper close by. And even though she'd helped Nikki eat the chocolate bar, she was still hungry. She dug through the pantry, found a bag of potato chips, and pulled it off the shelf with a triumphant yank.

"This'll work." She headed for the table.

I once had pommes frites in Paris.

"Millicent. Speak English. What on earth are *pommes frites?*"

I believe you refer to them as French fries.

Tara grinned. "Oh . . . yes. I actually had *pommes frites* for lunch today."

Ah, eating. I remember eating.

Tara shook her head as she sat down. "I adore you," she said softly.

For once, Millicent didn't have a comeback. But when Tara felt a gentle pressure all around her, she knew it was Millicent, giving her a hug in the only way that she could.

"You rock, Millicent," Tara said, then picked up her books.

She was just finishing up with her last bit of homework—writing a paper on Sinclair Lewis—when her cell phone began to ring.

She glanced at Caller ID before answering, because she had

no intention of talking to Flynn O'Mara today, and maybe never, but it was only Uncle Pat.

"Hi, Uncle Pat."

"Hi, honey. How was school today? Did you get a lot of questions about what happened?"

"You could say that," she muttered.

"Oh. Shoot. Was it bad?"

"You could say that," she said, and then sighed.

Pat laughed. "You're the best, you know that, don't you?"

Once again, she felt the love, which was just what she'd been needing. "Thanks. I needed to hear that."

"So, how about we go out to eat tonight? You pick."

"I thought I was grounded."

There was a moment of silence, then a sigh. "Not from me, you're not."

"Then yes, let's go. But are you sure we can afford it? It's another week until payday."

"If you don't make me buy steak, we're good to go," he said.

"How about pizza?" she asked.

"I'm assuming you're referring to The Hideaway?"

"Yes, please."

He chuckled. "Works for me. I'll be home in about an hour, but I'll want to shower before we go out. I smell like eight hours worth of garbage."

"Yuck. Are you sure you're not too tired to go?"

"No, I'm not too tired. I'm never too tired to take my best girl out."

She grinned. "I thought Mona was your best girl."

"She's just the girl of the hour. You're my best girl. Always."

"Thanks, Uncle Pat."

"See you soon," he said.

"Okay. Soon."

You need to wear that blue shirt and your tan shorts.

"Please. Millicent. This isn't a date. It doesn't matter what I wear to go out to eat with Uncle Pat."

It always matters what a lady wears when she goes out.

Tara frowned, doubting if ladies wore shorts when Millicent was alive, then nodded. Millicent might be a ghost, but she was the only female in her life who gave her advice.

"All right. The blue tee and the tan shorts it is."

Tara was just about to take her first bite of pizza. Hamburger and mushrooms. Yum. Her mouth was watering as she slid the corner of the slice between her teeth and bit. It tasted as good as it smelled.

"This is so good, Uncle Pat. Thanks for taking us out."

"My pleasure, honey," Pat said, as he dug into his pizza, too. "You've had a seriously stressful couple of days. It was the least I could do."

Tara shivered where she sat. It was amazing how good it felt to be appreciated.

"So, how's Flynn?" Pat asked.

Tara rolled her eyes. "Who knows?

Pat looked startled. "Did you two have a fight?"

"Not really, Uncle Pat. He's just scared of me and what happens around me, I think."

Pat nodded, as he continued to eat. "I can understand that. Can you?"

"As much as I hate to admit it . . . yes. But it still doesn't make it any easier to face."

"He'll probably get over it in a day or two."

"Maybe," Tara said. "But I might not. I don't have time for someone who runs hot and cold like water out of a tap. I have a life to live and I don't intend to worry about what some guy thinks about me, or whether I'm going to embarrass him or not."

"Good for you," Pat said.

"Just don't let my thing with Flynn mess you up with Mona. I know you like her a lot."

Pat nodded. "Yes, she's fun to be with, but I've backed up a bit on the dating. I'm giving her some personal time right now. Her ex is dying of cancer, and she's all confused about that."

"Oh. I didn't know that she'd told you," Tara said.

"You knew?"

"I picked up on it one day when Flynn and I were together."

"Well, it's a serious thing and she's confused about how she feels. I don't intend to add to the confusion."

"So we're both sort of single again, hunh?"

Pat grinned. "I'm good with it. How about you?"

"I don't really have any options," Tara said, and polished off her last bite, then reached for a second.

"They're going to have some sort of a service for DeeDee Broyles' remains," Pat said.

Tara was surprised. "Really? Who's doing it?"

"I heard it was Captain Farrell of the Stillwater Police Department. Said it was the least he could do for the lady who used to make cookies for his grandma."

Tara sighed. "That's really nice. If it's okay with you, I would like to go."

"I thought you might. That's why I mentioned it."

"Do you know when?" Tara asked.

"Not for sure, but I'll find out and make sure we both go."

"Thanks, Uncle Pat."

He winked, then waved at their waiter to refill their drinks and their meal continued. About an hour later, they left the Hideaway.

"I'm going to stop and gas up before we go home," Pat said. "I might not have time in the morning."

"Okay," Tara said, and kicked back in the seat to wait as Pat pulled up to the pumps at a quick stop.

She was watching traffic and the people on foot who were passing by when she realized someone inside was in trouble. She didn't know what was wrong until her uncle started to go inside to pay. All of a sudden, she flashed on someone holding a gun and knew the store was being robbed.

"Uncle Pat. Come back!" she screamed, and grabbed her

cell phone.

Pat stopped and turned around and came back. "I'm sorry. What did you say, honey?"

"Get in the car. Get in the car. The store is being robbed and we've got to move," she said, as she dialed 911.

Horrified, Pat jumped into the car and backed up into the shadows, but left the car running.

"911. What is your emergency?" the dispatcher asked.

Tara's voice was shaking as she rattled off the information. "The quick stop at Western Avenue and Highway 51 is being robbed. You've got to hurry. I think someone is going to get shot."

No sooner had the words come out of Tara's mouth than she and her uncle heard what sounded like firecrackers going off.

"Oh, Lord," Pat said. He hit the accelerator and peeled out of the parking lot, leaving rubber behind.

"Shots were just fired," Tara said. "We're driving away from the scene."

At that point, she and the dispatcher disconnected. She looked back just as two young men came running out of the store.

"Keep going, Uncle Pat."

"I didn't pay for the gas."

"We can pay later, but not if we're dead," she said.

His jaw clenched grimly as he kept on driving.

Two blocks down, she suddenly pointed. "Pull into that alley and kill the lights. Hurry!"

Thankfully, Pat didn't bother to ask why.

Seconds later, a red Jeep came barreling down the street behind them at a high rate of speed. Tara was on her knees looking out the back window and got a good look at the license tag as they flew past. She wrote the tag number down on her hand and then resettled herself in the front seat.

"Okay, Uncle Pat. They're gone. We have to go back," she said.

"You sure it's okay?"

"Yes. It's not like they're going to return to the scene of the crime or anything. Besides, I got their tag number and need to give it to the police."

Pat shook his head as he backed out of the alley, then once more, drove to the quick stop.

"I hope they had a working video surveillance system in place."

"I'm not sure it is, and the clerk is dead," Tara said.

Pat flinched. "Are you sure?"

She didn't answer. She didn't have to. The sick feeling in the pit of her stomach was all the verification she needed.

When they drove back to the station, police were already on the scene. One of the officers went to direct them away when Tara rolled down her window and held out her hand. She showed him the numbers she'd written on it.

"We're the ones who called in the robbery. I have the license number of the car they were driving," she said.

The officer had her out of the car within seconds and began taking her statement. One of the other officers on the scene happened to look up, saw her standing beside their car, and then headed toward her.

"Hey, kid. Aren't you the girl who found the body in your back yard?"

Tara nodded. "Afraid so."

"Did you just witness this robbery, too?"

"Afraid so."

He frowned. "I would not like to be your parent."

Pat came up behind Tara and put his arm around her shoulders. "Well, I would," he said.

Tara ignored the officer and continued giving her statement. "Uncle Pat was just about to go inside to pay for our gas when the shooting started. We drove away without paying, and Uncle Pat is all freaked out about that, too."

Pat nodded, then added to Tara's statement. "Officer, when you find out who owns the station, would you please give him our number and ask him to call so we can work out where I can send the money for the gas?"

"Sure," the officer said, made a notation on the pad on which he was writing, then continued to question Tara. "Did you see their faces?"

"Barely. All I know for sure is that they were driving a red Jeep and there were two of them. They were white. And they couldn't have been any older than in their twenties, although I'd guess younger."

"Could you pick them out of a line-up?"

"No, sir. All I got was their license when they drove past us."

He frowned. "They passed you on the street?"

"No," Pat said. "Tara told me to pull into an alley and cut the lights."

The officer frowned. "Do you always do what your kid tells you to do?"

Pat glanced at Tara and grinned. "In things that matter. And if you knew Tara, you would, too."

Tara stifled a smile. It felt good to be appreciated now and then.

As she turned around, she saw that a vehicle from the coroner's office had arrived. That job must suck. All they did was deal with the aftermath of someone else's mistakes.

A short while later, they were okayed to leave, and they drove home, a much quieter pair than they'd been when they left The Hideaway.

"I'm sorry the evening ended so badly," Pat said, as they pulled into the driveway.

Tara shook her head. "I'm not."

"Why on earth would you say such a thing?" Pat asked.

"Well, if we hadn't gone out to eat, and if you hadn't stopped to get gas, that robbery would have still happened, only no one would have witnessed it. The robbers would have gotten away with murder."

"I never thought of it like that," Pat said. "I guess you're right, although they would have had the security tapes, remember?"

"The cameras aren't real."

"You aren't serious?" Pat gasped. "You know, that's something I've never understood. Why the fake cameras? They aren't going to scare real robbers from doing what they're going to do, and they aren't needed for any other reason. Stupid. Just stupid."

Tara got out of the car, grabbed the box of leftover pizza and carried it into the house. She was putting it in the fridge as her uncle turned on the TV.

"Hey, kiddo, come look. We got home just in time for the evening news. I'm betting the story of Emmit's arrest is all over it."

And it was.

Tara watched with an odd detachment, knowing that tomorrow she was going to be treated differently than she had been today, yet accepting that in the long run, it didn't really matter. Even though her hottie boyfriend had done a freak, her BFFs had stepped up to the plate.

Could her lunatic world get any crazier?

Tara slept the night through without dreaming, but she knew as she got ready for school that the day was going to be much different than the one before. Last night's news had been non-stop about the discovery of a fifty year old crime scene at a house on Duck Street in Stillwater, Oklahoma. In fact, a news van from an Oklahoma City TV station was outside right now, but Uncle Pat was handling that. She'd done another freak when they'd knocked on the door this morning, but Pat had stepped outside with the reporter, leaving Tara to calm down on her own.

As she brushed her teeth, Pat gave the reporters the same line that she'd given everyone at school yesterday. As far as the general public knew, it was all a mystery to Tara and Pat, that they were just renters, but if the reporters wanted history or details into the story, they needed to talk to their landlord, Gene Whiteside, or to the police.

By the time she was dressed and ready to head out to

school, the news van was gone. She expected Uncle Pat to be gone as well, but to her surprise, he was still in the living room.

"Yikes! You scared me," Tara gasped. "I didn't expect anyone to still be here."

He picked up her backpack from the floor and held out his hand. "I'm giving you a ride to school. I can at least spare you the burden of having to deal with all the curious folks who might want to talk to you on the way."

Tara was filled with relief. "You are the best, Uncle Pat."

He grinned. "I have my moments. Come on, kiddo. I don't want you to be late."

"What about you?" she asked.

"I called the boss. Told him we were being hassled a little by the media, and I wanted to drop you off at school before I came in. He was great about it. So don't worry about me."

Tara nodded. It did feel good to let someone else carry the burdens now and then.

They got into the car and drove away. It wasn't far, so the drive was short. As they reached the corner on Husband Street where Tara usually met Flynn, it was noticeably empty. She wouldn't think about the pain of knowing how he'd bailed on her when the going got too tough. Flynn was a good guy. He just didn't know how to handle a girl who could see ghosts.

"Okay, here we are," Uncle Pat said, as he pulled up to the curb, leaned over and gave her a quick kiss on the cheek. "Have a great day."

"Thanks for the ride, Uncle Pat, and I will."

"See you later alligator," he said.

She felt his love all the way to her heart. "After while, crocodile."

She was still smiling as he drove away. Then she took a deep breath, turned to face the school building, and started up the walk. She felt the stares of the other students. Some waved. One even said 'hey.' But mostly the jeers and whispers from yesterday were gone.

Fair weather enemies make fair weather friends.

I know, Millicent. Thanks for the reminder. Tara's spirits lifted another notch. Millicent was a hoot. But she was right that people who switched from one side to the other on a moment's whim weren't the kind of people she needed in her life.

Today your friends will kiss donkeys.

Tara laughed out loud, which was a little weird since there was no one around her. She didn't bother to correct Millicent this time about getting the words wrong. She might have to adopt 'kissing donkeys' herself, at least when she wanted to keep her language clean.

She ran into Coach Jones just inside the door and knew he must be on hall duty. Otherwise, she rarely saw him. When he saw her walk in, he grinned at her and winked.

She smiled back, savoring his acceptance. Coach Jones was one of the good ones. He was also one of the few teachers at Stillwater High who hadn't freaked out when confronted with her abilities.

The fact that Tara was walking in without Flynn brought more attention than the dead body in her backyard. She caught startled looks, then heard whispering behind her back. But this wasn't the bad kind of gossip. This was just news. Someone had a fight. Someone wasn't dating someone else. Normal teenage stuff. Not the malicious stuff she'd had to cope with yesterday.

She was almost to her locker when a couple of guys came out of a classroom on her right. "Hey, Tara. How's it going?"

It was Corey Palmer, Nikki's hottie. Tara eyed the blue tips on his hair, then grinned. "Good. And you?"

He gave her a high-five. "Good to go. Hang in there. Oh, hey . . . have you seen Nik?"

"Not yet. I just got here."

"Dang. That girl won't answer her phone and she has my homework in her car."

Tara grinned. "Sorry."

"Yeah, me too," he said, and then headed down the hall.

By the time she got to first hour, she was feeling good about the day. No one had dissed her. She hadn't seen any lost or lingering wraiths, and Millicent hadn't sent out any ghostly warnings. Even Henry was absent.

She slid into her seat, then looked up, straight into Mrs. Farmer's face. Yesterday she'd judged Tara without knowing all the facts. Tara wasn't feeling all that kindly toward her.

Let it go.

Tara sighed. Millicent was right. Holding grudges never hurt anyone but the person doing the hating.

She opened her book, pulled out the paper she'd written on Sinclair Lewis and took it up to the basket on Mrs. Farmer's desk and dropped it in.

"Thank you, Tara," Mrs. Farmer said. "What did you think about Sinclair Lewis?"

"To be honest, Mrs. Farmer, after the last few days, nothing I've read could compare with what's been happening in my life."

Mrs. Farmer's face turned pink.

Tara turned around, returned to her seat and waited for class to start.

The boy who'd called her a crack head yesterday managed to mutter 'I'm sorry' as he passed by her desk. The two girls who'd laughed rudely were silent. Tara felt vindicated, but still somewhat sad. Once again, she was the odd girl out, the new girl at school who had yet to fit in.

Finally it was Friday. Homecoming. There would be a bonfire at the pep rally after school, then the football game would start at seven p.m. Tara didn't know if she was going to go, but she was pretty sure she didn't want to come face to face with Flynn and have him hurt her all over again. All week, they'd played at ignoring each other in every class and all over the campus, but she'd caught him looking at her a dozen times when he thought she wasn't looking. She'd done the same. Each time he'd caught her staring, she'd quickly turned away.

She couldn't get past how awful this was.

The last few days at school had been an eye-opener. Tara

had learned something about herself. She wanted Flynn back in her life. She just didn't think it was going to happen. Then Nikki, Mac and Penny had caught her on her way out of school Friday evening, offering to give her a ride to the bonfire.

"I don't know if I want to go," Tara said. "I don't want to run into Flynn and deal with a lot of drama."

Nikki made a face. "Forget Flynn. Just call your uncle and ask. It never hurts to ask."

"I guess," Tara said, and quickly made the call. When her uncle answered, she didn't wait for chit-chat. "Hey, Uncle Pat. Tonight is Homecoming and Nikki, Mac and Penny just offered me a ride to the pep rally and the game afterward."

"That's great, honey, just remember to be home by midnight."

"Thanks a bunch, Uncle Pat. You rock."

"See you later alligator," he said.

Tara eyed her friends and sighed. "After while crocodile," she mumbled, then disconnected.

Mac and Penny giggled.

Tara just shook her head. "You have no idea,"

Nikki just shook her head. "No biggy. My Dad still plays air guitar in the kitchen when he's helping Mama cook dinner."

Tara grinned. "Good to know I'm not the only one with a parent still locked in his past."

"So, can you go?" Nikki asked.

"Yes. I can go."

"Ace," Nikki said, and before Tara knew it, her night had been planned.

She was going to the bonfire—with her BFFs. And she was going to the football game afterward. And she was going to have a good time.

Tara felt like she was walking on air as Nikki dropped her off at her house. She needed to make sure her favorite jeans were clean, wash her hair, and . . . who knew? Maybe she would have fun after all.

Chapter Nine

Tara made a face at herself as she smeared on some lip gloss, then gave her dark hair a last sweep with the brush. She squinted at the mirror until she almost looked like Angelina Jolie, which made her feel as close to pretty as she ever did. She was wearing her favorite jeans and a gold t-shirt, which would be a great match to Stillwater's blue and gold colors. Nikki had warned her to bring a sweatshirt because it was supposed to get cooler tonight, so she had her dark blue zip-up hoodie by the front door, ready to go. She had ten dollars and the house key in her pocket, and was anxiously waiting for Nikki to swing by and pick her up.

When she saw her coming, her heart skipped a beat. *Calm down, Tara. It's just a pep rally.*

But it wasn't just a pep rally. It was a step into belonging somewhere, with friends. Two things that had been sadly lacking from her past were friends and a boyfriend. She no longer had a boyfriend, but she had a midnight curfew and money in her pocket. Things weren't all bad.

Nikkie swung into the driveway and honked. Tara grabbed her hoodie and locked the door on her way out.

"Where's Corey?" Tara asked, as she got into the car.

"He's on the team, remember? They're already there," Nikki said.

"Oh, right. Sorry. I'm not very good with sports."

Nikki grinned. "It's okay. You have *other* skills."

Tara laughed. "Don't remind me. I'm just hoping for an ordinary night."

"And hoping for a win, too."

"Right."

"So, first to the pep rally, then the game. Did you eat

supper?"

"No. I was too excited," Tara confessed.

"Cool. We can get dogs at the concession stand. They have good ones."

Tara nodded. "Are we picking up Mac and Penny, too?"

"No. Mac usually picks up Penny because most of the time I'm with Corey." Then she glanced at Tara. "Are you and Flynn still on the outs?"

Tara nodded.

"Don't worry. Stuff usually works itself out."

"Or not," Tara said. "Whatever happens, happens. I can't worry about something I have no control over, you know?"

"Totally," Nikki said, and down the street they went.

The pep rally was being held at the parking lot at Hamilton Field and when they arrived, it was already filling up fast. The pile of wood for the bonfire was huge, which explained the city fire truck parked nearby—obviously a 'just in case of emergency' backup plan.

Tara got out of the car and walked with Nikki toward the gathering of students around the woodpile. Nikki stopped every few feet to talk to someone different. Some of the kids Tara knew. Some she'd seen around campus, and some were total strangers, but all of them included her in the fun. By the time they got to the actual bonfire, Tara couldn't stop smiling. She saw Bethany and Mel and some of the other cheerleaders bouncing around the crowd with their pom poms, laughing and shouting back and forth to the kids who were gathering, keeping the mood high and the fun in gear. Prissy was standing within the perimeter of the crowd with a sad, wistful look on her face. Tara would have felt sorry for her, but the girl had brought every bit of her trouble onto herself. How wack was it to cheat? Beyond stupid, that's what.

She saw the guys on the football team, including Davis, Bethany's boyfriend, but she didn't see Corey.

"Hey, Nikki. Where's Corey?"

Nikki pointed. "There . . . just behind Coach Jones."

"Oh, yeah, I see him now. Look, he's waving at us."

Nikki's cheeks flushed, but she was grinning. "That's cause I blew him a kiss."

"Nice," Tara teased.

Nikki nodded. "Yes, he sure is."

"So, what happens now?" Tara asked.

"See Coach Jones? He'll make a little speech, and since Davis is Captain of the team, he'll probably light the fire. You'll figure the rest out."

"Cool," Tara said.

What happens with the pile of wood?

Tara was glad Millicent was there, too. *OMG, Millicent, how intense is all this? I'm having fun with people my own age.*

I repeat, the wood? What happens with the wood?

Tara glanced at the pile. *Oh. Right. They set it on fire.*

How pagan. Why?

Someone jostled Tara and smiled an apology. *I don't know exactly. Maybe just to get into the spirit of the upcoming game.*

You burn wood to play ball? That makes no sense.

Tara laughed. *You're right. It doesn't. But that's what makes it fun.*

Don't get too close.

Yes, Mother.

Actually, I have never had the experience of childbirth.

Millicent was so literal. *I was being sarcastic because you were treating me like a child.*

I knew that.

"Look, they're about to start," Nikki said. "The wind is going to blow smoke in our faces if we stay here. We need to move."

Tara was right behind Nikki one minute, and the next thing she knew, someone had her by the arm and was pulling her backward.

"Hey!" she yelled, and spun around. "Oh. It's you."

Flynn looked taken aback, but he didn't let her go. "I want to talk to you," he said.

Nikki heard Tara yell, then saw what was going on and smiled. "I'll see you in the bleachers."

Tara had no intention of letting Flynn O'Mara know how much she'd missed him. She folded her arms across her chest and glared. Even if he did look beyond hot, she wasn't letting him know.

"What do you want, Flynn?"

"You."

A knot formed in the pit of Tara's stomach. This was intense.

"I don't believe you," Tara said. "Nothing has changed in my life that will make me any easier to deal with."

"But something has changed in mine," Flynn said.

"Like what?" Tara asked.

"I found out I don't like how it feels to see you and not be able to touch you. I found out that no matter how mixed up your life is, mine feels empty without you. I found out that you're worth the trouble. That's what."

Tara felt like she was floating. No one had ever said anything that amazing to her before.

"Look, Flynn . . . I don't—"

"Well, I do," he said, and took her by the hand. "Give me another chance, Moon girl. Please."

Behind them, the crowd roared. Obviously the bonfire had been lit, but it had lost considerable significance for Tara.

Once, when I was in Paris, a Count broke my heart.

Not now, Millicent. Tara stared at Flynn.

He died before we could make up. I regret that.

Oh. *Point made. Advice taken.*

Tara pointed a finger at Flynn. "I don't expect someone to agree with everything I do, but it's not fair to diss me about stuff I can't control."

"Absolutely," Flynn said.

The cheerleaders began a cheer. The crowd was with them all the way. Tara, knew it must be great, because the cheers were huge when the cheerleaders had finished. She wasn't sorry she was missing it, though.

Smoke drifted into their eyes. "The smoke . . . we need to move," Flynn said.

Tara let him lead her toward the backside of the crowd. They walked until they were behind the fire truck. Away from the smoke—and the eyes of the crowd.

Flynn turned, waiting for her to say the magic words that he was forgiven, but she didn't budge.

"Tara?"

Tara sighed. "You so hurt my feelings."

Flynn leaned forward until their foreheads were touching, then he took her hands and pulled them around his back. "I'm really sorry. I didn't mean to. I guess I was just . . . "

"Scared?"

He nodded.

"Sometimes, I am, too," Tara said.

"Really?"

"Seriously. My life can be crazy . . . lunatic crazy."

Flynn cupped her face, then leaned forward. Their lips met. His firm and searching. Hers warm and accepting. When they finally pulled back, Tara was shivering.

Oh. My. God.

"Am I forgiven?" Flynn asked.

She nodded.

He smiled, then slid his hands beneath her hair and cupped the back of her neck. "Wanna go watch a big ole pile of wood burn?"

Tara grinned. "It's been my lifelong dream."

"Then who am I to deny my girl her dream?" Flynn took her by the hand and together, they walked back into the crowd. When they found Nikki with Mac and Penny, they had to endure some teasing about having had the shortest breakup in history.

Then Nikki punched Flynn lightly on the arm. "Just don't screw around with our BFF, okay?"

He nodded. "Definitely my bad. Just give me a break here."

"It's Tara's call," Nikki said.

"He's a good guy," Tara said. "Just a little misguided."

Flynn grinned. "So guide me, Moon girl. I'm yours."

They all laughed, which eased the last of the tension.

Tara felt like dancing. She couldn't remember being this happy in the longest time.

"You still hungry?" Nikki asked.

"Absolutely," Tara said. "Let's head for the concession stand before the game starts."

They trooped over to the concession stand, pooled their money and bought a round of hot dogs and soft drinks, and headed for the bleachers.

The sun set a few minutes after kickoff and took the warmth of the day with it. Tara grabbed her hoodie and zipped it up, thankful Nikki had cautioned her to bring it. By that time, her stomach was full, and her heart was filled with so many emotions she couldn't have identified them all to save her life. Every time Flynn looked at her, she saw past his face to the man he was becoming, and she liked what she saw. And even though she didn't understand half the rules of the game, this was turning out to be the best night of her life.

The Homecoming Queen was crowned before the game started and Tara watched the ceremony with interest. There were attendants, all from lower classes, and three contestants who were seniors. Each of the girls was wearing a fancy dress. Some of the dresses were short, some were long, but all of them sparkled like diamonds beneath the floodlights. Each girl was escorted by a member of the team.

The queen contestants were Bethany, her friend, Mel, and another girl named Justine, who Tara didn't know. The band played as the girls were escorted out onto the field. Nikki was talking a mile a minute, but Tara couldn't hear over the music. She just nodded and grinned and stuffed her hands into the pockets of her hoodie against the evening chill.

On the outside, Tara appeared to be tuned in, but inside, she'd gone quiet. She kept thinking that, but for the grace of God and her psychic abilities, the only ceremony Bethany might have been involved in during her senior year was a funeral—her own.

"What are you thinking, Moon girl?" Flynn asked.

"How pretty they all look," she said.

"Not as pretty as you," he whispered.

Tara felt her cheeks flush. "Thanks."

"Oh. Look. Bethany won!" Tara said, as they announced the winner.

She stood up and started clapping with the rest of the crowd, happy for the good turn of events in Bethany Fanning's world.

"Davis is gonna kiss her big-time," Nikki said. "Corey said the boys bet him he wouldn't do it, but he's determined."

Tara rolled her eyes. "Mrs. Crabtree will have a stroke."

They laughed, well aware of how on the mark Tara's comment was. Mrs. Crabtree liked things done properly, and laying a Hollywood kiss on one of her senior girls in front of the entire crowd did not fall into that category.

When it came time to put the crown on Bethany's head, Davis, as the Captain of the football team, crowned her quickly, then took her in his arms and, as Uncle Pat would say, laid one on her.

At first, everyone clapped, but when the kiss continued, the clapping morphed into hoots and catcalls. When the kiss kept going, laughter ricocheted all around the stadium. But the kiss didn't stop, and Tara could tell that the coaches were starting to get a little antsy. One of them poked another one and pointed, as if telling him to go out and stop it. But no one moved, and the kiss kept going, and suddenly, Tara got it. Davis was telling Bethany, in front of the whole town, that, despite everything she'd endured, she was still as important and desirable as she'd ever been. If her heart had been full before, now it overflowed

Then the band started playing, which was the signal for them to march off the field. But no one moved.

The crowd got quiet.

It was as if the whole world was holding its breath.

Suddenly, the crown Davis had put on Bethany's head slipped sideways, falling over her ear and conking Davis on the nose.

He yelped and pulled back.

Bethany grinned as she grabbed her crown and repositioned it on her head.

Sorry, but I couldn't take it any longer.

Tara almost choked. *Millicent! Did you make her crown slip?*

Somebody had to do something. I need a cold shower.

Tara would have thought Millicent would have loved such a romantic gesture. *You are so busted. You do not spoil a moment like that again.*

Doesn't mean I can't remember what passion felt like. Once when I was—

OMG. *Stop. I do not want to hear this.*

Whatever.

When Tara's ear popped, she knew Millicent was gone. But knowing Millicent, she wouldn't be gone long, and she wouldn't be far. Still, she'd done what needed to be done to get the show on the road. The contestants filed off the field with their escorts, and were ushered to a special place in the stands where the Queen and her attendants would "hold court" during the game.

"That was the best," Tara said.

Flynn grinned. "You mean what Davis did?"

"No. I meant Bethany getting crowned Queen. After everything she went through, I am glad some good stuff is happening in her life."

Flynn's smile slipped, as he realized what Tara was getting at. "Oh. Yeah. You are so right."

Unaware of their conversation, Nikki leaned over past Mac and Penny and tapped Tara on the knee. "It won't be long now," she said.

"To what?" Tara asked.

Nikki cracked up. "You are such a lunatic. To kickoff, girlfriend. This is a football game, after all, and we're playing Union."

Tara giggled. "Oh. Yeah. Right. Where's Union?"

"It's a high school in Jenks, which is close to Tulsa," Flynn said. "Ever been there?"

"Nope."

He grinned. "So, there's actually a place you and your Uncle Pat haven't lived?"

She laughed, and a few moments later the game began.

The roar of the crowd and the excitement of being in the middle of something so ordinary as a high school football game had Tara almost giddy. For the first time in her entire life, she felt like she belonged. It was, without doubt, her best night ever.

Stillwater High was ahead by one touchdown at the end of the first quarter and the crowd was amped. By the end of the second quarter, Union had rallied and the game was tied. The crowd was just one solid roar. Tara was worn out from the emotional ups and downs. She only understood half of what was going on, and never did quite get the hang of why the referees were blowing their whistles all the time, or why so many yellow flags kept getting tossed, but she did know when it happened, if it was against Stillwater, it wasn't good.

Finally, at half-time, the band took the field and the people in the stands began heading to bathrooms and the concession stand. Tara and Flynn were on their way to the concession stand when she began hearing one voice shouting louder than all the others. Flynn was talking to her, but she couldn't focus on him for the panic she heard in the voice.

"Flynn! Do you hear that?" she asked.

Flynn frowned. "I hear everything, Moon girl. What do you mean?"

"That woman. The one who's screaming. I think she can't find her little boy."

He tilted his head, then suddenly, he heard her, too. "Oh. Man. Yeah. She's totally freaking, isn't she?"

"Come on. She needs help."

Flynn followed Tara through the crowd, past the concession stand and toward the restrooms where a small crowd was gathering. A security guard had arrived and was talking to the frantic mother. Tara walked up just as the mother was explaining to the guard what had happened. Her voice was shaking and her face was streaked with tears.

"His name is Billy. He's six years old, but small for his age, with blonde hair and green eyes. He's wearing a Star Wars sweatshirt and blue jeans."

"When did you last see him?" the guard asked.

"Right here. He was standing beside me when someone ran into me and spilled the pop I was holding all over us. I was getting something out of my purse to clean us up, and when I turned around, he was gone."

Tara was uneasy. That sounded like more than an accident. Something told her it had been done on purpose to distract her so someone could snatch the child.

Without waiting to explain herself, Tara grabbed hold of the mother's arm and closed her eyes. The connection was instantaneous. She saw two people running, one was carrying a little boy who wasn't moving, which meant they'd done something to him to keep him quiet.

"Parking lot," she cried. "They're running through the parking lot. Hurry. Green Pinto. They're going to put him in a Green Pinto. It's parked at the back of the lot near the high school."

Flynn grabbed the guard's arm. "You have to believe her."

"No, I don't," the guard said. "Hey kid, turn the lady loose."

"Hurry!" Tara screamed. "If they get out of the lot, you'll never see him again."

The mother looked confused.

"You *have* to believe her," Flynn repeated. "If you want your son back, listen to her." He looked around for help. "Thank God. Tara, there's Detective Rutherford. In the concession stand line. I'll be right back."

Flynn ran over, grabbed him by the arm and dragged him toward the guard. "Tell him!" Flynn was shouting. "Tell the guard to believe her!"

"What's going on here?" Rutherford asked.

"Who are you?" the guard asked.

"Detective Rutherford, Stillwater P.D.," he said. "I missed the first half and just got here. What's happening?"

"My little boy . . . he got lost and I can't find him anywhere," the woman said.

Then Rutherford noticed Tara. He took one look at Tara's face and knew she was seeing something they couldn't.

"Where is he, kid?"

"The parking lot," Tara said. "At the back. Green Pinto. Hurry!"

"Call it in!" Rutherford yelled at the guard, and started running.

Once the connection was broken between Tara and the mother, she gasped. "Come on, Flynn. We have to help. They can't get away."

The crowd of people who'd been listening started running behind them. All they knew was to go to the back of the lot and find a green Pinto. Losing a kid was a parent's worst fear and everyone wanted to help.

Flynn, along with Rutherford and half a dozen men sprinted ahead. Tara wasn't far behind. Off to the right, she saw two police cruisers suddenly appear, blocking off two of the streets out of the parking lot, while another one sailed past with the siren screaming and lights flashing.

All of a sudden, Tara keyed in on panic and knew it was coming from the people who'd snatched the child. She felt their desperation and the darkness in their hearts.

Hurry, hurry, hurry. It was all she could think.

Then she began hearing shouts. Two more police cars appeared at the back of the parking lot. As she ran, she heard more shouts.

"Get down on the ground! Get down on the ground!"

And she knew the police had caught the kidnappers. She stopped running, letting the rest of the people pass her by, and leaned against the hood of a car. Her heartbeat was thundering in her eardrums and there was a pain in her side.

"I am so out of shape," she muttered.

A good corset works wonders.

Tara blinked. *Dang, Millicent, not that kind of shape.*

The child is fine.

Tara shuddered. Relief overwhelmed her. *What if I hadn't come tonight? Oh my God.* Before she knew it, she was crying.

It is not your responsibility to police the world.

Tara gulped, then shuddered on a sob. *Thanks, Millicent. You always seem to know the right thing to say.*

I will be reminding you of that statement the next time you berate me.

I do not berate. I do, on occasion, complain, but I'm not complaining now. Lord have mercy. This was so intense.

When she looked up, Flynn was coming toward her at a jog. She swiped at the tears on her cheeks and moved to meet him.

"The little boy. Is he okay?"

Flynn caught her on the run and hugged her. Tight. Without moving or talking.

Tara sighed. She got it. He was as emotionally moved as she was.

"Man, Moon girl. You rock," Flynn finally said. "And yes, the kid is fine. The cops think they used something like chloroform on him to make him quiet so fast, then pretended to carry him out the gate as if he'd just gone to sleep. Once they reached the parking lot, they started running."

"Did you see them? There were two, weren't there?"

He nodded. "Yeah, and that green Pinto had Missouri license plates. If they'd gotten out of here, they would never have found him, would they?"

She shook her head, then hugged him again. "Thanks."

"For what?" he asked.

"For believing in me. It was you who made it happen, you know. If you hadn't seen Detective Rutherford and gotten him involved, they wouldn't have believed me . . . at least not in time."

Flynn sighed. "Well, here's the deal, Moon girl. You haven't been wrong once since we met, so I'd be a fool not to believe."

"There goes the ambulance," Tara said, as it pulled out of the parking lot on the way to the emergency room.

"Yeah, they're taking the kid for a checkup, although he

was already coming to. Are you okay?"

"Sure."

"Think you can stand the second half of the game, or do you want to go home?"

Tara frowned. "No, I do not want to go home. I was having a great time until this. Since the little boy is okay, then so am I."

"That's what I'm talking about," Flynn said. "So . . . I don't know about you, but I need a cold drink. That's the fastest I've moved in ages."

"I was impressed," Tara said, as they started back to the stadium.

They were walking hand in hand when someone yelled Tara's name. She stopped and turned. It was Rutherford.

"Way to go, kid," he said, as he jogged up to them. "They ran a check on the men and came up with something pretty ugly. They're both registered sex offenders. The kid would have been in serious trouble if you hadn't gotten yourself involved. Like I told you a few days ago, I think you're onto something. You need to hang a shingle."

"And what? Start reading palms? Get serious."

He laughed, then glanced at Flynn. "You're fast, O'Mara. Are your grades as good as your feet?"

Flynn shrugged. "They're better than average, why?"

"Oh, I don't know. Something about you makes me think you'd be good cop material."

"Really?" Flynn asked.

Tara grinned. "That's amazing, because he's planning to go into law enforcement . . . of some kind. When he graduates, you might give him a good recommendation."

"Are you going into college first?" Rutherford asked.

Taken aback by the cop's interest in him, Flynn shuffled his feet, then stuffed his hands in his pockets. "Yeah. I want at least a couple of years and then I'll see if I still feel the same."

Rutherford clapped him on the back. "If you ever decide to go into law enforcement, give me a call. I can recommend a good academy."

Flynn's smile spread. "Thanks. I appreciate that," he said.

Rutherford walked off, leaving them on their own.

Flynn looked at Tara, then grinned. "That was quite a sales pitch on my behalf. Thanks . . . I think."

Tara grinned back. "Lunatic. Remember. Totally lunatic."

"So, let's go watch a ball game."

"Absolutely," Tara said.

They walked back into the stadium holding hands while talking and laughing about nothing in particular, happy another disaster had been averted.

Chapter Ten

The next morning Tara was still floating on air from last night. She had three BFFs. She and Flynn had made up. They'd saved a little boy from sexual predators. Bethany Fanning had been crowned Homecoming Queen. Stillwater High beat Union in the homecoming game by a teeth-grinding three points. Talk about stoked.

When she got home, she'd told Uncle Pat about everything three times, except, of course, the fact that Flynn had kissed her behind the fire truck at the pep rally, and again on the front porch when he'd brought her home.

Uncle Pat had his own brand of news to tell her, too. DeeDee Broyles' memorial service was going to be graveside at the cemetery that morning at 11:00. After all that, it had taken forever for Tara to go to sleep.

But morning had come, despite the adrenaline rush, and now she and Uncle Pat were hurrying through their regular Saturday chores—cleaning house, making grocery lists, doing laundry—all the stuff a mother would have normally been overseeing. It never occurred to Tara to feel sorry for herself. It was difficult to miss something she'd never had, and Uncle Pat was an amazing parent, even if he was a little stuck in the past.

"Are you through in the bathroom?" Pat asked, as he carried an armful of folded towels and washcloths down the hall.

"Yes. I'm going to get dressed for the service, but I don't know what to wear."

Pat looked blank. This was a question that rarely came up, and one he never had a good answer for.

"I don't know, honey. I would say, nothing weird."

She grinned. "So, that means my mini-skirt is out?"

The shock on Pat's face was comical. "You have a mini-skirt?"

Tara rolled her eyes. "No. That was just a joke."

"Oh. Well . . . I knew that," Pat muttered, and went into the bathroom.

Tara did a little skip as she crossed the hall into her bedroom and began digging through her closet. It wasn't like she had all that much to choose from, but she didn't want to diss DeeDee by wearing something inappropriate.

I'd go for your best jeans and something without wrinkles.

Tara frowned. *Was that a diss, or are you trying to tell me something?*

I am unaware of the word 'diss.' Are you trying to say 'this?'

No, Millicent. It's a shortened version of the word 'disrespectful.' Get it?

Then why don't you just say 'disrespectful?'

Tara rolled her eyes. *I am not having this conversation with you.*

Then who is it I am talking to?

Tara grinned. There were times when Millicent missed the subtleties of the current culture. *I will wear something without wrinkles.*

She heard a slight pop, like the sound of a bubble bursting, and then Millicent was gone, obviously satisfied that her suggestions were being followed.

Tara slid hangers across the bar, looking for something that would pass ghostly inspection. Finally, she settled on a white, long-sleeved shirt and her best jeans. She brushed her hair until it was shining like dark chocolate, pulled the sides away from her face and fastened them at the back of her head with a small, tortoise shell clip. She added a little lip gloss, and called herself good to go.

And, because they would be going to a cemetery, she made sure to wear her Saint Benedict's medal, just in case there were any lingering spirits who felt like getting pushy. Today was not the day to be swamped by any displaced spirits with a bad attitude.

She dropped her cell phone into her little black shoulder bag and headed for the living room to wait for Uncle Pat. While she was waiting, her cell rang. It was cool to get phone calls from someone other than Uncle Pat, and when she saw Caller ID, she grinned. Even cooler to get phone calls from a guy like Flynn.

"Hi, you," she said.

"Hi, Moon girl. How's it going?"

"Oh, okay. Uncle Pat and I are going to a graveside service for DeeDee Broyles this morning."

"Oh. Man. Sorry I didn't know. But, it wouldn't have mattered. I have to work until four this afternoon, bussing tables at Joe's."

"It's okay," she said.

"So, the reason I'm calling. Are we still on for tonight?"

"Yes. Are we still going to the movie?"

"Unless you want to do something else?"

"No, no, the movie is good. Uncle Pat and I don't go much, so I haven't seen anything that's playing. What are we going to see?"

"Why don't you check out the listings and times and call me back sometime today to let me know so I can pick you up in time."

"Will do," Tara said.

"Okay, Moon girl. See you later."

"Yeah, see you later," Tara said. She was still smiling when Uncle Pat came into the room.

"Does that smile on your face have anything to do with Flynn O'Mara?"

Tara grinned and blushed. "Maybe."

"So, I'm assuming that means you two have a date tonight?"

She nodded.

He just shook his head, and then gave her a hug. "My little girl is growing up."

Tara rolled her eyes. "Uncle Pat. I haven't been little in years."

"It's a figure of speech, missy. Are you ready to go do this?"

Tara sighed. "Yes. And for once, this is a good funeral, right?"

"Right, honey. It's about honoring a valiant little spirit." He glanced at his watch. "I guess we better get this show on the road."

A few minutes later, they were on their way. When they arrived at Fairlawn Cemetery, it soon became apparent that not many people were coming. But that stood to reason, since most of the people who would have been DeeDee's friends had either moved away or passed away. Tara knew it really didn't matter to DeeDee. She was finally where she needed to be.

A stocky middle-aged man stood beside the open grave with his hands in his pockets, staring out across the cemetery. When he heard them approaching, he turned around. His eyes narrowed as he zoned in on Tara.

Tara felt his shock and knew he still found it hard to believe in what she could do, but to his credit, Captain Adam Farrell didn't let it show. His focus shifted to her Uncle Pat, and he walked toward him.

"Adam Farrell," he said. "I'm guessing you are Pat Carmichael, and this would be Tara."

Pat shook the man's hand. "Yes, I'm Pat. Nice to meet you, Adam."

Tara smiled. "Nice to meet you, Captain Farrell. Detective Rutherford told us you used to know DeeDee."

Adam's expression softened. "Yeah. I was really little, but I spent a lot of time at my grandparents' house, which was across the street from what used to be the Broyles house. I was really sorry to find out what had happened to her."

"Emmit isn't ever going to get out of jail . . . is he?" Tara asked.

"No way," Adam said. "He confessed to murder. He's gonna die in jail."

"Good," Tara said. "He was scary."

Farrell frowned. "I heard. Next time tell someone."

"There won't be a next time," Pat said abruptly.

Tara wisely kept her mouth shut, and a few moments later, the hearse from the funeral home arrived, followed by a church van with the pastor who would perform the service.

Then another car pulled up behind the church van. Tara squinted her eyes against the morning sun, wondering who it could be. When Nate Pierce stepped out of the car and started walking toward them, she sighed.

Of course.

He helped find DeeDee. It stood to reason he might want to see her laid to rest, as well. He was wearing sunglasses as he came toward them. She had no way of knowing that his gaze was on her, alone—or that he was as puzzled by his fascination with her, as he was of what she could do.

"Professor Pierce. I'm glad you came," Tara said, as he walked up.

Adam nodded at Nate.

"Nice to see you, Pat said.

Nate shook Pat's hand. "Detective Rutherford told me about the service." Then he took off his glasses and stared straight into Tara's eyes.

Tara felt pinned by the intensity of his dark gaze, and stifled a shiver.

Nate started to lay his hand on the top of her head, for some reason he stopped and drew it back. His voice was soft, but intense as he looked her straight in the face. "You are one of the blessed ones, Tara Luna. It is my honor to know you."

Tara was so stunned by what he'd said she couldn't speak.

Then two more cars pulled in behind Nate's car and the moment passed.

Tara thought she had prepared herself for the ceremony, until six uniformed policemen got out of the two cars and solemnly marched to the back of the hearse.

"Oh . . . oh, wow," she whispered, as her vision blurred.

They all watched as six of Stillwater's finest, acting as pall bearers, carefully carried the mortal remains of DeeDee to her final resting place.

Tara knew that none of these men had even been born when DeeDee died, yet they gave her as much respect as if they'd been members of her family.

"That is so cool, Detective Farrell," Tara said softly. "DeeDee would be honored."

The ceremony began, and DeeDee was honored by a pastor who spoke as if he'd known and loved her. She was honored by Adam Farrell, who remembered a long-ago Halloween and the kindness of his grandmother's neighbor. She was honored by six officers of the Stillwater Police Department, who'd sworn to serve and protect the citizens, no matter who they were, or how long they'd been gone. She was honored by a man who'd used twenty-first century technology to find a young woman from the past whose future had been cut short.

Finally, she was honored by a teenager named Tara Luna, who cared enough to seek justice for her wronged and restless spirit.

It took less than an hour out of Tara's Saturday to come to the service, but it was something she would remember for the rest of her life. Later, Pat and Tara drove out of the cemetery without speaking, still wrapped up in the poignancy of the simple ceremony and the kindness of the man who'd cared enough to make it happen.

They were driving up Main Street when Pat reached out and gave Tara's knee a slight pat. "You okay, honey?"

"I'm fine, Uncle Pat."

"How about we grab a couple of burgers at the Sonic and take them home?"

"That would be great," she said.

Don't forget to order pommes frites.

Tara leaned back against the seat and smiled. *Yes, Millicent, I will eat French fries. Just for you.*

Yum.

"What are you smiling about?" Pat asked.

There was no way Tara was going into an explanation of

the mental conversation she'd just had, so she lied. It wasn't a bad lie. Just a necessary one.

"I was thinking about Flynn," Tara said.

Pat rolled his eyes. "Sorry I asked."

"Come on, Uncle Pat. He's a good guy and you know it."

"I know. I just don't like to think about another guy stealing my girl."

"Oh, Uncle Pat. No one can steal me from you . . . ever. I was yours first and nothing will ever change that."

Now Pat was the one blinking tears. "Thanks, honey." Then he pointed. "There's the Sonic. What are you hungry for?"

"One thing's for sure, I'm having French fries. And a cheeseburger with everything on it but onions."

He grinned. "Gotta keep your breath kissing fresh?"

"OMG. You did not just say that."

Pat was still laughing when he pulled into the parking slot and rolled down the window.

"Dr. Pepper to drink?" he asked.

"Absolutely."

"Coming right up," he said, then leaned out and punched the button to order.

The rest of the day went surprisingly smoothly. Tara called Flynn and told him which movie she wanted to see.

"Way to go, Moon girl. That was one of my choices, too."

"Good," Tara said. "So, is 7:15 too early for you? The other showing is at 9:45, and I'm afraid I won't make curfew if we go to the late one."

"The first one is good. I get off work at 4:00, remember?"

"Yeah, right." Then she added. "How's your Mom?"

"Doing okay. She went to see Dad yesterday. She hasn't said much since she came back, but I know it bothered her."

"I'm so sorry for what's happening."

"Yeah, me, too. I can't change what he did, but I'm not gonna let it pull me down."

"You rock, Flynn," Tara said.

"Thanks, Moon girl. So I'll pick you up about 6:45, is that okay?"

"Yes. See you later."

"Yeah. Later."

Tara was still wearing her best jeans, but she'd changed from the white long-sleeve shirt to the red and black top and the black hoodie Uncle Pat had bought her. She'd left her hair down because she liked the weight of it hanging against her back.

When she heard the knock on the door, followed by the sound of Uncle Pat's laugh, she knew Flynn was here. She gave herself one last glance in the mirror, then left her room.

"Hey, there she is," Pat said, as Tara entered the living room. "Wow, you look real pretty, Tara."

"You sure do," Flynn echoed.

Tara felt herself flushing, but the praise felt good. "Thanks, guys. I do what I can with what I have."

They laughed, and the awkwardness of the moment passed.

"We'd better be going," Flynn said. "Tara told you where we're going, right?"

Pat nodded. "Yes, to the movies, right?"

"Right."

"Have fun. Drive safe."

"Absolutely," Flynn said.

"I'll be home by midnight, Uncle Pat. If we have a problem, you know I'll call."

"See you later, alligator," Pat said.

Tara grinned. "After while crocodile."

And then they were gone.

They got to the movie in plenty of time to get popcorn, and they made it to their seats just as the lights were going down.

"Just in time," Tara whispered.

Flynn nodded, then grinned. "You gonna eat all that by

yourself?" he whispered.

Tara grinned, and put the popcorn between them as the movie began.

They laughed in all the right places, and flirted with each other during the slow spots. By the time the movie was over, Tara was pretty sure she was falling in love. She couldn't say for sure, because it had never happened before, but whatever it was she was feeling when she was with Flynn made her weak in the knees.

Remember what I've taught you.

Tara sighed. Just when the going got good . . . Millicent. *You didn't exactly teach me anything. You just bossed me around.*

Different way of saying that. Same results.

I remember everything.

Good. Leave them wanting and they'll came back for more. Give it away and they move on to greener pastures.

OMG, Millicent. You make me sound like a cow.

I assure you, that was not my intention.

When the lights came up, Flynn took Tara by the hand and led her out of the theater. "Are you hungry?" he asked.

"Yes, but it already cost a lot to go to the movies, and we bought popcorn. You don't need to spend all your money to make me happy."

"I was thinking Taco Bell?"

Tara laughed. "That I'll agree to."

"You're amazing, Moon girl."

She shrugged. "I'm just used to watching what I spend, okay?"

Flynn squeezed her hand and leaned close to her ear. "And I appreciate that."

"So, let's go ring Taco's bell," Tara said, laughing as they headed out of the theater and into the parking lot.

Flynn was laughing at her joke when out of nowhere a familiar wall of hatred swept over her.

"What is it, honey?" Flynn asked immediately.

"That sick feeling is back, and the rage that comes with it is so awful. I don't understand it. I can't key in on it, but it keeps getting to me."

"Come on, we're almost at the car," he said, and quickly got her inside and out of the parking lot.

The farther they drove from the theater, the better she felt.

"That was so bizarre," she said, and then shuddered. "Ugh. I can't describe how awful that feels. It's like I'm going to be sick to my stomach, or something."

"Are you sure you want to tackle Taco Bell? It's not exactly easy on a queasy stomach."

Tara managed a slight smile. "That rhymed. Way cool, Flynn. Easy on a queasy."

He shook his head, then laughed. "You're something," he said. "So, Taco Bell, here we come."

By the time they arrived, Tara managed to shake the feeling off sufficiently to do justice to a couple of tacos and some iced tea. Being with Flynn was so much fun, but the feeling in the parking lot had taken some of the joy out of the evening. She couldn't help but remember how Flynn had wigged out on her the last time she'd felt that rage.

She wanted to believe that was behind them, but she couldn't be sure. She lived a crazy life—a lunatic life—and it took a strong person to deal with it. Still, despite the bad feeling, tonight had been a blast, and it wasn't over yet. No need borrowing trouble before it came.

"Want another taco?' Flynn asked, as he finished off his fourth one.

"No way. I am so stuffed," Tara said.

Flynn glanced at the clock on the wall, then at Tara. "Wanna drive out to Boomer?"

"To the lake?"

Flynn nodded.

Tara's breath caught in the back of her throat. Was this where it ended? If she went, was he going to expect something she wasn't ready to give?

Flynn's eyes narrowed thoughtfully as he realized what she was thinking. "Relax, Moon girl. I'm not pushing, and I'm not expecting anything from you but your company."

She sighed. "Sorry. I'm just not—"

Flynn grabbed her hand. "Never apologize for what you want . . . or don't want. Never. Do you hear me?"

All the tension went out of her at once. "Then yes, but I'm gonna go to the little girl's room before we leave, okay?"

"Absolutely," he said. "I'll be at the door."

Tara headed for the bathroom without further concern. She trusted herself, and she trusted Flynn to keep his word.

I'll be in the back seat, you know.

Tara rolled her eyes as she went into the bathroom. *Of course you will. Do you need to go into the stall with me, too?*

Sarcasm does not become you.

Then stop treating me like a five-year old.

Sorry. I'm still on the clock.

OMG, was she serious? *You are so not being paid to keep tabs on me.*

Go pee and stop arguing, please.

Whatever!

Tara was still fuming when she came out, but she didn't let on. Flynn would want to know what could have possibly happened in the bathroom that would have made her angry, and she didn't want to have to explain that Millicent would be riding shotgun in the back seat.

Flynn held up a small sack as they went out the door. "Dessert."

"Yum. Are those cinnamon strips?"

"Yep.

"Double yum."

"So, let's go watch submarine races, what do you say?"

Tara giggled. It was what kids said when they went out to the lake to park. Like anyone could see submarines racing underwater. And like they would even be looking at the water when everyone knew they would be making out.

They got in the car and started out toward Boomer Lake. The scent of sugar and cinnamon filled the inside of the car as Flynn popped a CD into the player. Within moments, Kenny Chesney's sweet country voice lulled Tara even more.

"I love his stuff," Tara said.

"Yeah, me, too," Flynn said. "He's puts out a good vibe, you know?"

"Absolutely," Tara said.

"Talk to me, Moon girl. Tell me things I don't know about you."

"Except for the fact that I see and talk to ghosts, I am so not interesting."

"That's your opinion, honey. Talk. Like what's your favorite color? What's your favorite holiday? Things I would have known about you if we'd grown up together, you know?"

"Oh. Yeah. I get it. So, I will if you will."

"Deal. You first."

"Um . . . my favorite color is blue. I love pecan praline ice cream and I take my Oreo cookies apart and lick the icing first. Halloween is my favorite holiday, for reasons you can imagine." She grinned. "I mean . . . what other time can my spooky friends come out to play without freaking people out, you know?"

"Are you serious?" Flynn asked. "Like, people could see them?"

She nodded. "Sometimes. What about you?"

"Favorite color . . . red. Favorite holiday, Christmas. My favorite food is the meatloaf and mashed potatoes that my Mom makes."

"Oh. My favorite food is fried chicken."

"Can you cook?" Flynn asked.

"Are you kidding? Yes. How else would we eat? Uncle Pat is fair at cooking, but he's better at reheating. The problem is, he mixes stuff up when he reheats it, which I hate. I like to know what it started out to be, even if it's leftover."

Flynn laughed out loud. "Yuck."

Tara nodded. "Seriously yuck."

They were still talking as Flynn turned off the highway and onto the road leading out to the lake. A few minutes later, he pulled up to a boat dock, then killed the engine, but left the CD playing.

"Wanna get out?" he said. "It might be a little cool."

"I've got my hoodie," she said.

He rolled down the windows, letting Kenny Chesney's voice out into the night. "So, let's go."

They walked hand in hand to the dock. Flynn moved behind Tara, put his arms around her, pulled her close against his chest and rested his chin against her head. They stood without moving or talking, just watching the half-moon glow on the dark surface of the water while the music swelled with the accompanying calls of frogs and whippoorwills. An owl hooted off to their right, and somewhere in the distance Tara heard a coyote yip.

She sighed. Absolutely perfect.

Then Flynn suddenly turned her loose and turned her around to face him.

"So, Moon girl . . . may I have this dance?"

Tara's heart skipped a beat, then she walked into his arms. They began to move, swaying to the music beneath the pale glow of a harvest moon on the battered boat dock at Boomer Lake. They danced through three songs, and even when the music was fast, they stayed in a slow, two-step pace as they fell farther and farther in love.

When the last song ended, Flynn stopped.

Tara looked up. His face was shadowed, giving him a different, almost scary good grown-up face. Her heart stuttered. *He's going to kiss me. And I am so going to kiss him back.*

She put her arms around his neck.

It was all the urging Flynn needed. He lowered his head. Their lips met, briefly at first, barely touching, then he kissed her again, a little longer, a little harder.

Tara sighed and leaned into his embrace.

When he finally stopped, he gave her a last kiss on the forehead, then brushed a lock of her hair away from her eyes, tracing the shape of her cheek, then her lips with the tip of his finger. His voice was as soft as the breeze around them.

"You are so beautiful, Tara Luna."

"Oh, Flynn," she whispered. Her heart was hammering so

hard she could hardly think.

Then Flynn groaned, and instead of kissing her again, hugged her hard and swift.

"I think it's time I took you home," he said.

Tara nodded, too moved to speak.

He took her by the hand and led her back to the car. "We didn't eat that dessert," he said, smelling the cinnamon sugar on the fried strips of flour tortilla as they got in.

"I just had mine," Tara said.

Flynn grinned, more than pleased by what she'd said. "Thanks, honey," he said. "I guess I did, too."

He started the car and headed back into Stillwater. They were comfortably quiet as Flynn drove down Western Avenue, when all of a sudden, Tara got that sick, ugly feeling again.

Whoever was causing this was close. She turned around and looked over her shoulder, but there was nothing to see besides the headlights of dozens of cars coming and going.

"What is it?" Flynn asked.

"That feeling is back," Tara said.

"Damn," Flynn muttered. "Have you told your Uncle about this?"

"No."

"Don't you think you should?"

"What do I say? I get sick to my stomach every now and then, but I don't know why? Knowing him, he would think I was pregnant. If I tell him I feel disembodied rage, he'll totally freak. He might not ever let me leave the house, especially after what happened with Emmit Broyles."

Flynn frowned. "I don't like this."

Tara flinched. Was this where he freaked out again? "Neither do I. I'm the one getting nauseated, remember?"

"Yeah. I didn't mean it like that. I'm just worried about you, okay?"

She relaxed. "I know. It's creeping me out, too."

The feeling followed them all the way to Duck Street, and all the way into the driveway, even though the street was deserted. Tara paid close attention as she got out of the car and as Flynn was walking her to the door, but didn't see any cars parked nearby, or any passing traffic.

"Is it gone yet?" Flynn asked.

"Yes. I wish I knew where it was coming from."

"You're sure you're okay?"

She nodded. "Yeah. But I'm glad Uncle Pat's home."

"Good. Safe and sound, then," he said, as she put her key in the lock. "I had an amazing time."

Tara smiled. "I did, too. Thanks for everything."

"Absolutely," Flynn said, and one more time, they went into each other's arms.

The kiss was sweet, but less intense than it had been at the lake, which was good. Tara was still trying to regain her good sense.

"Night, honey. I have to work until closing tomorrow, but I'll call you tomorrow when I get a chance."

"You better," Tara said, and then stood on the porch until he got in the car and backed out of the driveway.

When she walked into the house, she was pleasantly surprised to realize the sick feeling had faded fast. This whole thing was confusing.

Then suddenly, she realized she'd left her purse in Flynn's car, and it had her cell phone in it.

"Dang it," she muttered.

Suddenly, she saw car lights coming back up their drive. She peeked out the window. It was Flynn. She hurried out on the porch only to be hit once again by that sick feeling as Flynn came running up.

What was going on?

"You forgot your purse," he said.

Ignoring the nausea, Tara pasted on a grin. "I didn't do it on purpose, but you've just earned yourself a second goodnight kiss."

"That's what I'm talking about," Flynn said, as Tara kissed him soundly.

"Thanks so much for bringing it back."

"Trust me, it was my pleasure," Flynn said, and then

headed back to the car.

He drove away, and just like before, the feeling faded.

Weird. Too weird.

Tara locked the door behind her and headed to the kitchen to get a cold drink before going to her room. She was getting a Dr. Pepper out of the fridge when Pat came into the kitchen carrying a glass. Her first thought was that he was drinking again, but when he bent down and kissed the side of her cheek, all she smelled was Dr. Pepper.

"I thought I heard you," he said. "Was that Flynn coming back?"

"Yes. I forgot and left my purse in the car. I'm sure glad he saw it because my cell phone was in it."

"Did you have a good time?" Pat grabbed a couple of cookies out of the cookie jar on the cabinet, then sat down at the table.

"The best," Tara said. "The movie was funny. We ate tacos at Taco Bell, then went dancing."

Pat grinned. "Wow. You did have a night of it. So, tomorrow you can sleep in. Glad you're home."

"Me, too. Night, Uncle Pat," Tara said, and gave the other man in her life a goodnight kiss, too.

Pat picked up his cookies and headed back to bed. "Sleep well," he said, and left her in the kitchen.

Tara topped off her Dr. Pepper, and was on her way down the hall when something hit her. Something so startling that it sent an instant shaft of panic straight to her heart.

OMG.

She kept trying to remember if she'd ever felt sick when she was by herself. There hadn't been a single time. Every time she'd felt sick, she'd been with Flynn. She'd just assumed all this time that the rage was aimed at her. But just a few minutes ago when Flynn had driven away, the feeling had gone with him. Then when he'd come back, it had too.

OMG. OMG.

What if the rage wasn't aimed at her after all?

What if it was Flynn who was in danger?

Just when she thought everything about her life was turning normal—at least for her—had another mystery appeared? And if so, how was she going to make it go away? She had to figure this out before someone—like Flynn—got hurt.

Where did Tara's Adventures Begin?

My Lunatic Life

Excerpt

Four days later, the dark shadow came back.

It was three minutes after four in the morning when Tara woke up needing to go to the bathroom. She was on her way back to bed when she sensed she was no longer alone. Her heart skipped a beat as the darkness between her and the hallway moved into her room. A normal girl's first instinct would have been to scream or run away, but Tara was used to spooks. She stomped into her bedroom with her hand in the air.

"Look, Smokey . . . I'm bordering on PMS, so you don't want to mess with me. State your business or make yourself scarce. And don't go *through* me again to do it. I'll tell Henry and Millicent to kick your behind so hard you'll never be able to put two ectoplasmic molecules together again. Do you read me?"

The shadow shifted then disappeared through the floor.

"That's better," Tara muttered, then headed to the dresser, where she'd left her jewelry box. She dug through it until she found her Saint Benedict's medal, fastened the chain around her neck, and then crawled back into bed. "Like I don't already have enough to deal with," she said wearily, then punched her pillow a couple of times before settling back to sleep.

All too soon, the alarm was going off and another strange day was in motion.

The first week at school sped by without further trouble. At home, Uncle Pat got cable hooked up to the TV and internet to Tara's laptop. She caught up on episodes of *Glee* and *Gossip Girl*. She was beginning to believe everything was smoothing out. Then week two came, reminding her she was still the new kid in school.

Tara was on her way to first period when she turned a corner in the hall and came up on the cheerleader trio who she now thought of as The Blonde Mafia. Prissy saw Tara, then pointed at her and said something that sent the other two into a fit of giggles.

"You are so lame. You're almost as funny as your name," Prissy said, as Tara walked past.

Tara rolled her eyes. "Is that rhyme supposed to pass for white girl rap?"

Prissy's face flushed angrily as kids standing nearby heard it go down and started laughing, but Tara didn't hang around for a second stanza. She didn't have time for their petty crap. She walked about ten feet further down the hall when she heard a shriek and turned just in time to see two hanks of Prissy's hair suddenly standing straight up on either side of her face like donkey ears.

Millicent! Tara stifled a grin. "I knew that was gonna happen," she said, and kept on walking.

Tara's first-period teacher was at her desk, poking frantically at the screen of her smart phone. She looked up when Tara walked in, nodded distractedly, then returned to what she'd been doing. The air was so thick with distress that Tara immediately sensed what was wrong.

Mrs. Farmer had money troubles.

That was something she understood. She and Uncle Pat rarely had an excess of the green stuff, themselves. And considering that his new job with the city of Stillwater involved reading electric meters, they weren't going to get rich this year, either.

She slipped into her seat, then took her book out of her backpack, trying to concentrate on something besides the misery Mrs. Farmer was projecting. But for a psychic, it was like trying to ignore the water while going through a car wash. Tara was inundated with wave after wave of her teacher's thoughts and emotions.

All of a sudden she knew Mrs. Farmer's husband drank too much. Her mother was a nag. Her sister was married to a doctor, which made her own husband's problems seem even worse. And suddenly Tara knew something Mrs. Farmer did not.

It wasn't that Mrs. Farmer couldn't manage her money. *Someone was stealing it.*

The room began to fill with other students, and a few minutes later the bell rang, signaling the beginning of class. Tara felt Mrs. Farmer trying to focus on her job and Tara tried to do the same. English was one of her favorite classes.

"Good morning," Mrs. Farmer said. "Your assignment over the weekend was to read the poem, *The Female of the Species,* by Rudyard Kipling, then write a one-hundred word paper on it. This morning we're going to read your papers aloud in class."

The collective groan that followed her announcement was no surprise. Tara sensed that half the class hadn't even read the poem and of the ones who had, less than a dozen had completed the assignment. Tara pulled out her notes but had a difficult time focusing. She kept keying in on Mrs. Farmer's plight.

She knew what needed to be done to help her, but it meant making herself vulnerable.

The hour passed, and when the bell rang students scattered, even as Mrs. Farmer was still giving them their assignment for tomorrow. Tara had argued with herself all through class, when she really hadn't had an option. If she'd seen someone stealing, she would have told. Knowing it was happening and who was doing it and not telling was the same thing to her. She waited until the last of the students were gone, then headed toward the front of the room, where her teacher was erasing the blackboard.

"Mrs. Farmer, may I speak with you a minute?"

Unaware anyone had lingered behind, Mrs. Farmer whirled around, startled. "Oh, my. You startled me, dear. I didn't know anyone was still here. You're Tara, right?"

"Yes, ma'am." Tara sighed. There was nothing to do but jump in with both feet. "I need to ask you something, and then I need to *tell* you something."

She could see the confusion on her teacher's face, but she had to hurry or she'd be late for second period.

"Who's Carla?" Tara asked.

"Why . . . that's my babysitter," Mrs. Farmer said. "She stays at my home during the day and takes care of my twin daughters. They're only three."

"Okay . . . I need to tell you that she's stealing money from you. She's taking blank checks out of the new pads of checks in the box and forging your signature. That's why you're account stays overdrawn."

Tara could see all the color fade from her teacher's face. Mrs. Farmer gasped. "How do you know this?"

Tara sighed. "I just do, okay?"

Mrs. Farmer grabbed her by the arm. "Do you know Carla Holloway? Did she *tell* you this?"

"No, ma'am. I asked you who Carla is, remember? Uncle Pat and I just moved here, remember? We really don't know anyone."

"Then how . . . "

"Maybe I'm psychic, okay? When you go home this evening, get out your new checks and look through the pads. You'll find a couple of checks will be missing from each one. Confront Carla. She'll fold. And don't forgive her to the point of letting her keep babysitting for you . . . because she's using the money to buy drugs."

"Oh dear Lord," Mrs. Farmer gasped, and reached for her

cell phone.

Tara ducked her head and made a run for the hall. She'd done all she could do. The rest was up to Mrs. Farmer.

She made it to second period just as the last bell rang. That teacher frowned as she slid into her seat. Tara heard a soft masculine whisper from behind her.

"Good save, Moon girl."

She turned. Flynn O'Mara grinned at her. Tara rolled her eyes and then dug her book out of her backpack, trying not to think about how stinkin' cute Flynn was. Kind of had that classic heartthrob look, but with more muscles and straighter hair.

Henry showed up about fifteen minutes later and began trying to get Tara's attention. She sent him mental signals to be quiet, but he wasn't getting the message. Just before class ended they heard a loud commotion out in the hall. It sounded like doors banging—dozens of doors—against the walls. Henry threw up his hands and vaporized. That's when she realized whatever was going on out in the hall might have something to do with Millicent. The door to her classroom opened and flew back against the wall with a loud bang. The fact that it seemed to have opened by itself was not lost on the teacher or the students.

"Wait here!" the teacher cried, and dashed out into the hall.

Moments later Tara heard the fire alarm go off. The teacher came running back into the room.

"Walk in an orderly line and follow me!" Students grabbed backpacks and folders and fell into line behind her as she strode quickly out the door.

Tara's stomach sank as she slid in between Flynn O'Mara and a girl with blue hair.

"It's probably nothing," Flynn said over her shoulder.

Tara shivered. She knew better. It was something all right. It was Millicent. But why?

The halls grew crowded as students filed out of the classroom and made for the exits. To their credit, the exodus was somewhat orderly. As soon as they reached the school grounds, security guards began directing them to the appropriate areas. In the distance, Tara could hear sirens.

She kept looking back toward the school building. What had Millicent done?

Henry appeared in front of her, as if to say *I told you so*, then disappeared just as quickly again. A pair of fire trucks pulled into the school yard. Firemen jumped down from the rigs and hurried into the building. As Tara watched, smoke began to pour out of one of the windows on the second floor.

OMG! Millicent had set the school on fire? Why would Tara's lifelong ghost pal set the school on fire?

The moment she thought it, Tara heard Millicent's voice in her head.

I didn't set the fire. It was already burning between the walls. Give me a break. I was trying to help.

Sorry, Tara told her.

As if that wasn't enough drama for the day, a loud rumble of thunder suddenly sounded overhead.

Ghosts couldn't control the weather, so this wasn't Henry or Millicent's doing. A strong gust of wind suddenly funneled between the school and the gym. She shuddered. Even though the day was warm, that wind gust was chilly. Then it thundered again. She looked up at the underside of the building storm clouds, frowning at how dark they were getting.

"Are you cold?" Flynn asked.

She turned to find him standing right behind her.

"A little. Who knew we'd need jackets today? It was in the nineties when I left home this morning."

"Take mine," he said, as he slipped out of his denim jacket and then put it over her shoulders.

"Then you'll be cold," she said.

"Nah. I'm good."

She slipped the jacket on. The warmth from his body still lingered in the fabric, giving her a momentary impression of how it would feel to have his arms around her. It was an image that made her blush.

The wind continued to rise, with thunder rumbling every few minutes.

Tara shivered nervously as she looked up at the clouds. She hated storms.

"We're going to get soaked," she muttered.

A shaft of lightning suddenly snaked out of the clouds and struck nearby, sending the crowd into a panic.

"Into the gym!" Coach Jones yelled.

He waved his arms and pushed kids toward the gym.

"To the gymnasium!" a teacher echoed, and the crowd began to move. When the next shaft of lightning struck, this time in the football field nearby, they began to run. And then the rain came down.

Tara ran as hard as everyone else, but the ground was getting muddy and more than once she lost traction and slipped. If she fell, she would get trampled before anyone knew she was even down there. No sooner had the thought gone through her mind than her feet went out from under her. She was falling and all she could see were the legs of hundreds of students aiming straight for her.

Suddenly, Flynn pulled her upright. "Hang on to me, Moon Girl!"

She grabbed hold of his hand. Together they made it into the gym. They were heading for the bleachers before they realized they were still holding hands. They turned loose of each other too quickly, then grinned for being so silly.

"Thanks for your help," she said, and took off his jacket. "It's soaked. Sorry."

"It'll dry. Are you okay?"

"Yeah. Sure. Thanks again."

He eyed the dark hair plastered to her head and the wet t-shirt she was wearing as his grin widened. "You might wanna keep that jacket for a while." She looked down, then rolled her eyes. Everything—and she did mean, everything—showed, right down to her blue bra and the little mole next to her belly button.

"Perfect," Tara muttered. "Just perfect."

"Yeah. I agree," Flynn said.

She thumped him on the arm and then crossed her arms across her chest.

"Stop looking," she hissed.

"I'm trying, but hey ... don't blame me for an appreciation of the finer things in life."

Tara laughed despite herself, then put his jacket back on and climbed the bleachers. She sat down a little away from a crowd of sophomores and began wringing the water out of her hair.

I like her, Flynn thought. *I like this crazy girl.*

Flynn paused. If he followed her up and sat down beside her, it would only intensify what he was already feeling. There was no pretense with her. She was a little odd and definitely different from the other girls in school, but he had plans for his last year of high school that didn't include getting messed up by another female. Bethany Fanning had done it to him big time over the summer, and he wasn't in the mood to go through another dose of female drama. Still, something told him that Tara Luna wasn't fake, and if there *was* drama in her life, she wasn't the kind to exaggerate it.

He felt someone push him toward her, but when he turned around, there was no one there. Frowning, he climbed the bleachers and then plopped down right in front of her. That way he was close, but not staking out territory.

Tara had seen Millicent give Flynn a push. So, Millicent wasn't satisfied with playing havoc at school today. Now she was playing matchmaker.

I delivered him. You do the rest.

"I can do just fine on my own, thank you," Tara said beneath her breath.

Flynn frowned. "Sorry. I didn't know you'd set up boundaries. Want me to move?"

"No. No. Not you. I wasn't talking to you. Sit here ... wherever you want. Sorry."

Flynn's frown deepened as he looked around. "Then who were you talking to, if not to me?"

"Ghosts," Tara said. "I was talking to ghosts."

"Yeah, right. Whatever. I can take a hint." He got up and moved away.

Now see what you did.

"Just stop meddling," Tara snapped.

Whatever, Millicent said, echoing Flynn, then made herself scarce.

Tara slumped. Could this day possibly get any worse?

ABOUT SHARON SALA

Sharon Sala's stories are often dark, dealing with the realities of this world, and yet she's able to weave hope and love within the words for the readers who clamor for her latest works.

Her books repeatedly make the big lists, including The New York *Times*, *USA Today*, and *Publisher's Weekly*, and she's been nominated for a RITA seven times, which is the romance writer's equivalent of having an OSCAR or an EMMY nomination.

Always an optimist in the face of bad times, many of the stories she writes come to her in dreams, but there's nothing fanciful about her work. She puts her faith in God, still trusts in love and the belief that, no matter what, everything comes full circle.

Visit her at http://sharonsalabooks.com and on Facebook.

CPSIA information can be obtained at www.ICGtesting.com
Printed in the USA
LVOW11s1515100715

445789LV00001B/91/P